KADE

The $ecret Billionaire $ociety

BOOK 6

NANCY PENNICK

Allison-Hayes Publishing

ISBN-10: 1-7347996-5-X
ISBN-13: 978-1-7347996-5-1

The Secret Billionaire Society series is dedicated to my family who have loved, helped and supported me through this process.

PROLOGUE

"Mr. Kade Phillips," the voice said over the speakers.

The man behind the mirror had finally called my name. Wait! What the hell was I thinking? I was the only one left. He *had* to call my name.

We'd never met him, this man behind the mirror. We didn't know what he looked like. Yet, my friends and I agreed to put our lives in his hands and trust him. We only knew his code name—Mr. Smith. The name was definitely an alias or just a phony, made up on-the-spot moniker.

Smith was now in charge of us, the Secret Billionaire Society, which started as a joke in college. Funny thing, each of us made the Forbes Top100 list at one time or another in the past decade. Our friend Beau Miller also had a personal goal to make the top ten black billionaires in the U.S. before turning thirty. He'd achieved his objective last year, and if all went well, the Society would stay on those lists for years to come.

When I heard my name, I shifted nervously in my seat. The weight of the world fell on my shoulders. They depended on me, my band of brothers, to bring it home. Finish the job. But damn, I couldn't guarantee it.

Funny how Smith chose my buddy Gabe Nichols and me to be the last two. We'd met at the age of ten when we joined travel soccer, continuing to end up on the same teams in school and rec leagues until our junior year of high school. Then we committed solely to our high school team and set our sights on scholarships. A career-ending injury in the last game of the season ruined Gabe's hopes of a collegiate career. Sadly, the only offer I'd received came from a two-year junior college. Dreams dashed; we agreed to find our way outside the soccer world. Gabe wanted to work in the creative field of technology, and I just wanted to do something creative.

We realized we needed an excellent education and business background to succeed in whatever field we chose. Gabe kiddingly said we should go to Harvard. "Can you picture two Denver kids tearing the place up?" he'd asked me.

I'd immediately hopped on my laptop and searched for requirements to get into the school. "We can do this," I had said.

"I thought you wanted to model and make some money before going to college," Gabe joked, receiving a punch to the arm from me. Modeling. A major sore point in my life.

Through the years, many people suggested I should model, even strangers on the street. They'd stop me and say, "Your hair, those eyes. You'd be perfect." But my goal in life wasn't to pose for the camera. I wanted to get behind it, take the photos, learn the trade. Once I did, the sky was the limit.

The rest of the guys had met at Harvard their freshman year. Nash and Beau shared a dorm room while Chase and Finn lived down the hall in another. Gabe and I never encountered them until sophomore year. We'd all moved into the same apartment complex.

I'd met Finn in the apartment's laundry room and got to talking. I probably started the conversation, couldn't help being friendly. And for once, I didn't hear I should be a model. Yeah, guys told me, too, but Finn was different. He talked about his goals in life and wanted me to meet his like-minded buddies. I hesitated. I didn't go anywhere without Gabe or leave him in the dust. "If I can bring my best friend and roommate, you've got yourself a deal." I had told him.

"Go on," Gabe told me when I was ready to leave later that day. "I've got stuff to do."

I'd replied in a stern tone, "Don't pull that shit, Gabe. You think Finn wants his guys to meet only me, but you're wrong. We're a package. I told Finn you were coming, too. If they don't like you, I would never hang with them."

Gabe had called me Magnet for years. He said I attracted people like bees to honey, and not just girls. I didn't see it. I thought they were being friendly. Maybe he was right about the popularity thing, but I wanted to meet Finn's friends. I needed to discover why Finn appeared so driven at nineteen years of age.

How did we become the Secret Billionaire Society? A joke turned into reality. Chase and Finn were its first members. Nash didn't need much coercing to join, but Beau took a while. He wanted to make it on his own. Nash explained over and over that the group would let no one down, including Beau. They'd always be there for each other. After he'd thought it over, Beau joined the group.

Gabe and I were the last two holdouts. We were the artistic types who wanted to go into our rooms, close the door and create. The SBS, short for Secret Billionaire Society, heard our reasons for not coming on board and explained why we should. The biggest reason? Money. How could we do what we wanted without it? By junior year we were all part of the Society.

The guys made a deal on graduation day, knowing if we didn't, we may never see each other again. We came from all parts of the country and would need to make an effort to see each other. We agreed to celebrate our birthdays on one chosen day each year. No matter where we were or what we'd been doing, we'd dropped everything and showed up at the designated time and place. Every year turned out the same. Party until the wee hours of the morning, pass out and wake with a hangover. But the thirtieth celebration turned out differently from the other birthday bashes. *Much* different.

On that fateful birthday night, we drank, sang and reminisced until one in the morning. All went well until someone had gotten melancholy and began to ask if this was all there was to life—partying, drinking and making money. Nash stood, beer in hand, and gave quite the speech about the qualities of those three exact things until somehow a wrestling match ensued. We needed a way to shut him up or he'd ramble all night.

Out of breath, we finally gave up and sat on the floor. Staring at each other for the longest time, Chase, our unofficial leader, had said, "We need to do more than party, guys. We have the means to help people. We should make a pact, right here, sitting on this damn floor, to make a difference."

Finn, Chase's college roommate, was the first to respond. "Hear! Hear!" he'd said. "To Chase and the rest of us making the world a better place."

Nash joined in, and Gabe and I had held up our beer bottles. "Six," we all chanted our motto. "From the bottom to the top."

Beau had designed a special pyramid as the Billionaires' symbol. Our secret code. Only we knew its meaning. We'd even incorporated it into our business logos. Whenever we'd received the emoji, we knew someone needed help or a conference call would take place.

Right before the sun rose on our thirtieth birthday celebration, Beau had found someone named Mr. Smith to work with us. Gabe kept whispering to me or taking me aside to talk as Beau discussed details with the person on the phone. "Who'd accept an assignment without meeting us or believe the ridiculous premise we gave?" He'd glared at me, hoping his words had sunk in. "Obviously, the guy on the phone," I'd answered with what probably looked like a drunken goofy smile.

"But don't you think he has his own agenda?" Gabe growled.

"Let's see how it plays out," I'd said.

"Plays out?" Gabe had given me a look of horror. "We are entrusting ourselves and our livelihoods to someone we met on the phone! You're okay with it?"

The alcohol had loosened our inhibitions and trust factor. We were riding high and confident as hell. Well, maybe not Gabe. He never drank like the rest of us and was the first one awake the next day.

"Sure." I'd nodded at his question, trying not to laugh at the ridiculous look on Gabe's face.

"We already give sizeable amounts of money to charity, Kade," Gabe had said through gritted teeth.

"But this is Mission Impossible!" I'd replied. "Don't you want to play?"

"Play?" Gabe had thrown his hands in the air, giving up with a huff, and returned to the group where Beau continued negotiating with Mr. Smith.

"Gabe will change his mind once this starts," I had told myself. I'd always had a bit of wanderlust in me, leasing apartments in several cities and abroad. I never put down roots or built a house or a vast estate like the others. This plan, Mission Impossible, was something I'd never encountered in all my journeys. It appealed to me in so many ways. I was up for the challenge.

The guys had gathered around Beau, and he switched his cell to speaker so we could hear. I rushed to join them, not wanting to miss a thing. Somehow, Beau had convinced the man it wasn't a prank and asked him to be our mentor. Well, not exactly a mentor. Our silent partner, the guy you never see, like in Mission Impossible. He would give out the assignments. And that was how Mission Impossible was born.

Nothing was ever simple. Smith had an agenda. His biggest stipulation? He'd receive what we owned if we did not follow through with the assignments. It was to be our motivation, get our money back from him. If one failed, we all did.

We thought Smith had selfless goals when we hired him that night, spouting how much he liked our idea of doing something for the greater good. He promised to fit our assignments into our lives. Maybe he didn't have selfless goals after demanding our assets go into a nameless trust. He could end up with all our money, but the Society agreed we wouldn't quit the project. We'd succeed no matter the obstacles. Dare I say we *were* too drunk to make monumental decisions, just as Gabe suggested? Yet, that night I wholeheartedly believed in the mission.

Before ending the call with Mr. Smith, he'd instructed the six of us to put together dossiers. A special courier would pick up the flash drives and deliver them to Smith. Once he had the memory sticks in hand, he'd know everything about us. We'd requested separate assignments. Each man wanted his own mission. He could set the parameters, make the rules.

After Smith received and read our bios, he sent instructions via another messenger. Mr. Smith took no chances and didn't want us to use our cell phones, email, text, or any technical means of communication to contact him.

After our initial call, the first message we received said to build a soundproof room where we'd meet. That was how the bunker was born. A trusted contractor built the place on Chase's property, a two-room soundproof dwelling which looked more like a ranch house than a military operation. Mr. Smith could slip into a special entrance directly connected to the darkened side of the one-way mirrored room without being seen. The outer waiting area was the typical man cave with an enormous TV screen mounted on one wall. Loungers, a bar with comfort food, and the latest tech gear filled the rest of the space.

We'd get our instructions from Smith in the interrogation room, as we came to call it, and a burner phone, like Chase had, whenever we needed to speak to the man. Smith had already tweaked the rules for the other guys' missions after Chase's protests. He fought for the rest of us to keep our real phones, besides the burner, a lesson he'd learned from the first assignment.

So, back to my assignment. What did I have to lose? For starters, my leases on the apartments. Then my investments and bank accounts. How did I become a billionaire? Trusting Chase Young's investment skills. Yeah, I modeled during college and after graduation. I needed the money. But I listened to the people around me who did the other jobs, right down to food service.

Once I'd made enough cash, I handed it over to Chase. All of it. I trusted him.

From the money I'd made, I could buy into movie companies, produce shows and direct. Over the years, I looked for people who wanted to do the same and offered them a hand. In fact, right now I was helping a fledgling designer get his foot in the fashion door. Not an easy thing to do.

I'd trusted my friends twice. Once to join the SBS. The second when I handed my hard-earned cash over to Chase. What was one more time?

A sound jarred me from my thoughts, an unfamiliar voice, bringing me back to the present.

"Mr. Phillips?" the voice called to me again.

CHAPTER ONE

Mia Takeda stared out the apartment window watching for her best friend and design partner, Jordan Reese. He promised he had a lead. A good one this time. A mentor. A backer, he'd said. She'd put her life on hold to follow her dream. One which seemed to be fading fast.

"Oh, Jordan! Please, make it real," Mia whispered as she walked back to her drawing table.

Mia and Jordan had moved to New York City three years ago. "If we're going to make it, we need to move to the city," Jordan had told her. "I can't go without you, Mee. Please say you'll come. Let's agree to a five-year plan. If we don't make it by then, we'll give up. Well, I'll never give up and I don't believe you will either."

The pair had hunted for a cheap apartment in Greenwich Village, wanting to live in an artist community. Walking through the streets made them feel as if they were somewhere special and things could happen. Coffee shops, delis, and cheap hangouts told them they'd found the right spot.

Once they found a government-subsidized apartment in an old, drafty brick building, the hard work was complete. They had a place to live. They agreed to make the living room into a work area and placed two artist desks, which were secondhand drafting tables, close to the window to get as much natural light as possible. A sofa and table with two chairs took up the rest of the space. Two bedrooms, a kitchen and bathroom completed their home.

Mia flipped through her sketches, pausing at the ones she designed a few weeks before. She ran her finger over the title, *An Orange Ball*. She'd written it above each dress when she finished. Mia smiled at the memory, looking at the names she'd given the gowns according to the instructions. Vanessa. Missy. Rosa. After the event, she'd searched the internet and found the women who wore her dresses to the charity ball. The thrill was indescribable.

Jordan's mentor, who Mia had yet to meet, gave him a task to test his skills. Three designer gowns. One week to complete them. Jordan passed the job to Mia, claiming he didn't have time to work on the dresses. His sketches for their fall/winter collection needed his full attention.

According to this mentor, their line would debut during spring fashion week. Mia wondered if Jordan told the truth or exaggerated. Getting into a show that big with no credentials seemed impossible. Jordan was good at embellishing a simple story and perhaps made more of his encounter with his mystery backer than he should have. Regardless, she'd finished her drawings and had the time to work on the gowns. If the mentor liked them, he'd sponsor Jordan and Mia plus secure a spot for them during spring fashion week. A huge get.

Mia tapped her lips with a sketch pencil. "I need to talk to Jordan about our brand name. He said to leave the marketing to him and work on the creative end, but I am just as capable of doing both like he is." She put an elbow on the table, placed her head in her hand and gazed out the window. Reflecting on their past, it always astonished her how far she and Jordan had come, without him discovering she came from a wealthy family. One that could fund their entire dream.

* * * *

"Knock, knock, I'm home!" Jordan called as he opened the door. "It's ungodly hot outside." He fanned his face with one hand. "Not much better in here."

"It's July. What do you expect with no air conditioning?" Mia teased. "I have all the fans on," She stared at Jordan. "Is your shift over?"

Jordan had gotten a job at the local coffee shop soon after they moved into the apartment while Mia worked from home. She'd started a freelance business doing design work for online companies. It didn't bring in much income but paid the bills.

"Yes, finally. At least the coffee shop has air conditioning." Jordan held up a cardboard cup holder. "Our daily constitutional. I brought you an Americano. Iced."

"Thanks."

"Mee?"

Mia glanced up and noticed Jordan had snuck up on her, coffee in hand. He was a handsome man, clean shaven, oval-shaped face, firm jaw, bright blue eyes. He'd changed his hair from the popular silver gray to a bleached-blonde last week, and she didn't know which she preferred. *Actually, I like the natural Jordan with the light brown hair.* "Yes?"

"Um." He bit into his lower lip. "You know how I've asked everyone to call me Jor*dan*?"

"Emphasis on the Dan," Mia said with a roll of her eyes.

"Come on! We agreed you'd call me that in public," Jordan said as he poked her in the side.

"Stop!" Mia edged away from him with a giggle. "Please don't say I have to call you that all the time."

"No. We are Jordan and Mia. Always."

"That's a relief." Mia smiled at him. "You're my best friend. My confidante. I don't want it to change ... ever."

"The same." Jordan held out his hand, and Mia ran her palm along his.

"Okay, so what do you want to tell me?" she asked.

"This is for business only. I want to spell my name with a capitalized D. That way everyone will say it correctly."

"Or they might say Jor. Dan. Two separate syllables." Since Jordan looked so serious, Mia suppressed another giggle.

"It's a start, right? And we have time to decide. Well, not that much time."

"I'm glad you brought up names. We really need to solidify ours. I still like Fashion by Jordan and Mia. It sounds good. Rolls off the tongue."

"Yeah, I guess." Jordan lifted a shoulder.

"No." Mia knew him well. She pointed at him, dropping her jaw at the same time. "You want our brand to be JorDan! No way. We are equal partners."

"Come on, Mia. We've tried! J&M will remind people of another company. JorMee sounds like a baby tropical storm. "And," Jordan said with a sigh. "Jora or Dana just doesn't cut it."

"Who said we have to use any of those names?" Anger flared up inside of Mia. She didn't know why. They were only having a business discussion like they always did. She inhaled and let it out slowly to calm herself. "Remember how we'd sit in the dorm for hours writing out all kinds of names?" She shook her head. "If you want my opinion, plain and simple is the way to go. Jordan and Mia."

"Let's table the discussion for now. I have a lunch date. I came home to change my shirt."

"Did you meet someone at the coffee shop?"

"Yes. He's only in town for a day or so I need to get going."

"Did you introduce yourself as Jor*dan*?" Mia tried not to smile.

"What do you think?" Jordan narrowed his eyes. "I told him I'd show him around Greenwich."

"Ooh, have fun."

"You should get out more." Jordan rubbed her back. "I worry about you."

"I date."

"Rarely."

"I had boyfriends."

"One at school and two here. Although that one guy barely counted. Ralph?"

"Rafe." Mia waved him off with her hand. "Go. You're interrupting a creative moment."

"I thought you finished the collection."

"I am done. Just working ahead."

"Get. Out. You are working on a spring/summer book?" Jordan peered over her shoulder.

"No peeking." Mia covered her drawings with her arms. "When you get back, we'll lay out all of our fall/winter and see what needs tweaking. This can wait."

"It's a date. We'll go out to dinner, too." Jordan kissed her cheek. "Love you, Mee."

"Love you, too." Mia smiled and returned to her drawings.

Once Jordan left the apartment, Mia went to her bedroom. Just big enough to hold a twin bed, an antique dresser and nightstand, she'd filled the walls with beautiful copies of artwork and empowerment posters. One stark black and white was her favorite. *You are your only limit*, she read.

Luckily, for the size of the room, she had a decent size closet where she kept all her belongings. Mia had packed every fashion notebook and drawing pertaining to couture into two pieces of carryon luggage with wheels, making them easy to take wherever she lived. Organized by year, she could quickly find the files she needed. Mia had lugged the two pieces with her since the day she left home.

Before she dug into her history, Mia felt her stomach rumble and realized she was hungry. "What time is it?" She glanced at her phone to see it was well past noon and placed a lunch order. They would deliver it within the hour.

Mia popped open the carryon which held her older portfolios. On top were sketches from her fine arts classes in middle school. She rummaged through the pile until she found the sketch book marked, "Florida State".

"Oh, Van, I was in awe of you." Mia hugged the book to her chest and wistfully reminisced. "I was this young girl from a protective family, and you helped me find a new, stronger version of me. I never told you because it took years to become that person. I was very shy back then. Once I left school, I never saw you again. I'm sorry we didn't stay in touch. When I saw you wearing the dress I designed, my heart swelled with pride. Vanessa Alverez had made the society page. Still, I couldn't bring myself to contact you." She dropped her head. "Besides, you were so popular you've probably forgotten about me."

During Mia's elementary school years, she did quite well. In third grade, she surpassed the other children in every subject by leaps and bounds. The school called about her outstanding test scores and convinced her parents she should skip a grade. They didn't need much prodding and quickly agreed. She'd been nine, overly shy, and started the new school year as the youngest in the fifth-grade class. No one wanted to be friends with the little girl who was smarter than them. During this time, she'd lost herself in art and discovered she had a passion for design. When she entered middle school, her parents encouraged her to take Fine Arts and Art Appreciation. They had no idea she wanted to draw and create. They just wanted her well-rounded.

Mia had secretly researched design schools over the years. She dutifully applied to all the top schools in the country to appease her parents and to keep them from discovering her actual plan. Each college that received her application sent Mia an acceptance letter. Her father rejoiced and said the world was her oyster. After discussing her possibilities, Mia stole off to her room feeling sick. She sat on the edge of the bed, knowing she'd have to do as her parents said. Choose one of those schools. She was only sixteen. She'd turn seventeen in May but still underage and unable to make her own decision.

Choosing her own college would give Mia a taste of freedom. For once, she wanted to take charge of her education. Her parents had invested heavily in her schooling, both financially and emotionally and would balk at any change to their plan, yet something inside her told her to fight, stand up to them for the first time in her life.

A brilliant idea came to her. She grabbed an old textbook and opened to the map section, turning pages until she found what she wanted. Closing her eyes, Mia let her finger drop onto a map of the U.S. When she opened her eyes, she discovered her finger had landed on Florida. It didn't take long to find a few colleges she liked, and she quickly applied to one.

Once she'd received the acceptance letter, Mia recalled running out to the solarium to tell her parents she wanted to go to Florida State, a respected research and learning institute in its own right. Shocked, they'd thought she'd already chosen one of the ivy-league schools. An argument ensued. Mia pleaded with them, asking to get her way this one time. After speaking in private for what seemed like hours, her parents miraculously consented. They called her into the room and said they'd agree to her demands if she viewed it as a "gap" year, a break before "real" college. Mia quickly said yes to the proposal.

By August, Mia was on a flight to Tallahassee and Florida State before they changed their minds. The following spring, she'd turn eighteen and as an adult they had no jurisdiction over her. She planned to follow her dream and go to a design school. Her clever plan had worked.

While at Florida State, Mia applied to every prestigious design school in the country. Her parents weren't pleased when she dropped the news. A top design school accepted her into their program based on her work. Her parents stood their ground, insisting she choose another school from the list of ivy-league colleges which had accepted her. When she didn't, they refused to pay tuition. Luckily, she'd saved her money, and thanks to Jordan, she discovered she was good at waiting tables. They both were on a wait staff at a high-end popular restaurant during the years they attended school.

When Mia arrived at the design school, she'd met Jordan Reese. He had a vibe about him. Everyone wanted to be his friend, yet they'd chosen each other as best friends. They'd found themselves in the same classes, snickered at the same jokes and were good at sending silent messages to each other. As the months continued, they became closer and closer. Mia had come out of her shell that year. Praise from the teachers and other like-minded students encouraged her. Those years were some of the best.

Mia's parents had hoped she'd fail at the design school. They thought her need to draw was childish and were quick to point out not many make it in the fashion world. Instead, she thrived. When they saw how well she did, they finally gave in and supported her choice, even offering to pay tuition. By then, Mia was used to taking care of herself and refused. She'd make it on her own or not at all.

The second year of school, Jordan had suggested they become a team. "With our looks? People will see we ooze style." Mia smiled at the memory. Her self-confidence was still in rollercoaster mode, so to have Jordan at her side as a partner made her feel she could conquer anything.

"We were young and stupid," Mia mumbled as she paged through her Florida State sketches. Most were basic and some showed promise. A lot of the models looked like Vanessa. Mia chuckled, holding one out to study it.

The buzzer rang, distracting her from her trip down memory lane. "Lunch is here." She hopped from

the floor, shut the door behind her, leaving the mess
for when she returned.

Mia walked to the front door, pushed the button
to let the delivery person in and waited. The building
had no elevator and they were on the third floor. It
could take a few minutes. The expected knock came,
and Mia opened the door to see one of the hottest guys
she'd ever laid eyes on standing on the other side. His
amber eyes and mysterious good looks, messy curls and
lean, muscular figure were the perfect characteristics for
a male model. *I've got to stop thinking in terms of models all
the time!*

"Oh!" The man's eyes widened. "Um, sorry, I have
the wrong ... you're ..."

No, please tell me he's not going to say it! "Japanese-
American?" Mia asked in an indignant voice, stopping
him before he went through a list of all the Asian
countries. "And yes, I speak English. I am fourth
generation and just as American as you are." She
thought she caught a smile in his eyes as they crinkled
at the corners.

"Would you like to know my nationality, too? It
would put us on even ground." The edges of his
luscious mouth twitched. "All I really know is I'm part
Scot."

Mia's mind immediately went to him wearing a kilt.
"I'm sorry. I get defensive sometimes." She winced at
the harsh words she'd spoken.

"Do people really think you don't speak English?"
he asked.

"Living here? With all the tourists coming and
going? Sometimes," Mia said with a sigh. "Well, not too
often, but something just happened ... never mind ...
I'm projecting."

"If I may, I'd like to finish what I *was* about to say."

"Sure, go ahead." Mia glanced at his hands. The man held no restaurant bag, so he definitely wasn't bringing her lunch. *Who is he?*

"I'm looking for Jordan Reese. This is the address he gave me. When you opened the door, I thought I had the wrong apartment. I was going to say, 'You're not Jordan Reese.'"

I love that he says Jordan without the emphasis on the Dan. "Sorry, again. I would like to start over. I'm Mia Takeda, his …"

"Assistant? He might have mentioned he worked with someone." The man wrinkled his brow. "I'm Kade Phillips. I'm helping Jordan with his career."

His career? What about me? "Oh?" Mia widened her eyes. "You're his mentor? Please come in." *I'll straighten this out. You need to know, Mr. Kade Phillips, that Jordan has a partner. Me!* She stepped back to let him inside, planning to straighten him out as soon as she could.

CHAPTER TWO

Kade could have stared into Mia's dark brown eyes all day. He blinked to focus and found her scowl had changed to a smile. "Thanks." He stepped past her into the room. "I'd like to start over, too. Hi," he extended his hand. "I'm Kade Phillips, here to see Jordan Reese. I have some important news to tell him."

"You can tell me," Mia answered. "I'm his partner."

"Oh? He never mentioned he had one."

A creased line formed along her brow. "Really?"

"We've only spoken a few times," Kade said, trying to smooth the line he caused on her pretty heart-shaped face. "I'm sure he planned to tell me."

"Where are my manners!" Mia touched the side of her head. "Can I get you anything?" She nervously looked over her shoulder at the kitchen. "I'm not sure what's in the fridge. In fact, I thought you were my lunch delivery."

"Sorry." Kade chuckled and held out his hands. "I've got nothing. Hey!" he said as if he'd had a lightbulb moment. "I have an idea. Why don't I take you to lunch and you can tell me what I need to know about Jordan and Mia."

"I promise I won't be so grumpy after I've eaten," Mia joked. "There's a good deli down the block. Is that okay?"

"Sounds great." Kade followed Mia out the door, studying her petite figure as she went down the stairs. She'd barely reached his shoulder if they stood next to each other. Her silky raven hair hung halfway down her back and bounced from side to side as she walked. He wished he could reach out and touch it.

Kade watched her from behind as they went down the three floors of steps. Mia held her own from the start. She'd opened the door to a stranger and took no prisoners. Assuming he judged her, which he hadn't, Mia stood up for herself. When she discovered Jordan never mentioned her, she set him straight. He liked that.

A thought blindsided him. *I like her. No, it seems different, like something I've never felt before. I'm captivated by her.* Surprised by this fresh development in his life, he struggled to gain composure. Kade Phillips didn't do girlfriends. He dated. If he eventually found the right someone, great. If not, he was fine with the way things were in his life.

They entered the deli, chose a booth towards the back and settled in. Mia kept staring at him, making him a little self-conscious.

"I'll come right out and ask," Mia said with a roll of the eyes. "It sounds lame to say it aloud, but were you ever a model?"

"You're kidding, right?" Kade gave her a hard time.

"Ooh, people ask you all the time, don't they? Forgive me?" Mia cringed. "In my defense, I was asking on a professional level. Remember, I design clothes for them to wear."

"Makes sense." Kade nodded to the waitress who'd put down the two turkey wraps they'd ordered on the way in. "Yes, I have modeled. Strictly for the money. Never wanted to make it my profession." He grinned at her. "You could model, too."

"Nope. Too short." Mia returned the smile.

"True. I sized you up on the walk over here. Very short." Kade feigned a scowl and shook his head.

"Hey! I'm five-four. Not that short," Mia answered him in a teasing way.

"Tell me about you," Kade said. "Besides being short and a fashion designer, what else do you do?"

* * * *

Mia couldn't get enough of his smile, the way he quirked his eyebrow when he teased her and those mesmerizing tiger-like eyes. *Am I falling for him? The fake delivery guy? No! Too soon. Remember Rafe?*

Rafe had swept Mia off her feet for three months last winter, then ghosted her like she never existed. Afterward, hurt and distrust followed her everywhere. Mia avoided casual conversations with any guys, yet Kade was different. It felt like a magnet drew her toward him. No matter how hard she tried, she couldn't stop looking at him, wanting lunch to never end.

"Well?" Kade tilted his head. "*Is* there more to your story?"

"Oh, there's always more." Mia blinked and stared at her plate. "But some things are mine and mine alone." She looked up and gave him a bright smile. "Plus, the rule is to never reveal too much about yourself at first. Keeps them guessing."

"I like that." Kade nodded. "Let's start with the simple stuff then. I'm originally from Denver, Colorado. My best friend is Gabe Nichols."

That caught her attention. "Of Nicholworks?"

"You've heard of him?"

"Who hasn't? How do you two know each other?"

"Soccer."

Mia dropped her shoulders and gave Kade a 'be serious' look. "Don't tell me you play soccer, too?"

"Not anymore. We met in rec soccer when we were ten."

"Oh! That's nice to have a friend from your childhood."

"We roomed at Harvard, too." Kade sipped his water, gazing at Mia over the edge of his glass. "Your turn."

"I grew up in California," Mia said.

"It's a big state." Kade smirked.

"San Jose area." *I can't say Atherton, one of the richest neighborhoods in America, can I?*

"It's nice around there."

"Have you been?" Mia hoped to distract him and not reveal exactly where she lived.

"I've been a lot of places. A vagabond of sorts."

"A vagabond who can sponsor our brand," Mia teased.

"Public or private school?'

"Private."

"College?"

"A year at Florida State, then on to design school. It's where I met Jordan."

"He's not your boyfriend?" Kade pointed at her.

"No." Mia wrinkled her brow. "He's not into me."

"But you're into him?" Kade quirked the eyebrow again.

"Do I have to spell it out for you?" Mia asked.

"I guess so."

"Jordan is gay."

"He never told me."

Mia liked that. Kade was refreshing, accepting of people. "Jordan never told me how you two met."

"I like to visit up-and-coming artist shows. We both stood in front of the same painting, tilting our heads, trying to figure it out." Kade laughed. "We got to talking. He told me how he dreamed of becoming a fashion designer. I always like a new project, so I asked to see his work. Those dresses he made for the charity ball sealed the deal."

I made those dresses! Mia decided not to say a word in fear of losing their backer. "I'm happy to hear."

"I know we just met," Kade said. "But I'd like to see you socially. That is, if you're not seeing anyone. And you probably are."

"Is that your roundabout way of asking me on a date?" Mia asked, lifting the corners of her mouth.

"Yes, it is. Dinner tonight?"

"I promised Jordan we'd work on the collection this afternoon. He said he'd take me out to dinner afterward."

"I don't want to get in the way of the creative process." Kade held up his hands. "Damn! I forgot! It's the reason I came to see Jordan."

"Can you tell me?" Mia asked.

"Yes." Kade nodded. "I secured a spot in the new designer category for Fall Fashion Week. They hold it elsewhere and not at the same time. But it was too good to pass up. Can you be ready?"

Mia's heart pounded. "We can't use the same designs. We're working on fall/winter and have to switch to spring/summer."

"I know and I'm sorry. But." Kade lifted a shoulder. "It's the best I can offer. Sometimes you must work under pressure. It' part of the business."

Overwhelmed, Mia fought back tears and straightened in her seat. "I better finish up here and get back to the apartment then. Jordan and I have a lot of work to do."

"I'll walk you back. Will Jordan be there? I want to break the news to him."

Mia bit into her bottom lip and could only nod.

* * * *

I feel like the biggest shit right now! Damn Smith. No wonder the guys curse and swear when they hear his name. Did I say they must work under pressure? Of course, I did! It's the only way this mission will continue to its crazy conclusion. Kade watched the look on Mia's face change from happy and smiling to a deer in headlights. They were having such a good time, but the mission got in the way. *At least she doesn't know who I am.* It was one consolation. He wanted Mia to like him for being Kade Phillips, the mentor. Not billionaire Kade Phillips.

As they mounted the apartment building's steps, Mia said in a quiet voice, "You'll need models. Good luck finding any at this late date."

At first it sounded like she was talking to herself, but Kade picked up on the message. "I'll get to work on it."

Before they entered the apartment, Kade gently placed his hand on her back. "I still want that date. Please think about it."

Mia said nothing and opened the door. Sprawling out on the living room's hardwood floors, Jordan lounged on his stomach with sketches all around him. He looked up in surprise when he saw them. "Greetings, Captain." He saluted. "I see you met Mia."

"You better clean this up," Mia said with a sweep of the hand. "Mr. Phillips has bad news."

Jordan rolled to his side and into a sitting position, while giving Mia a look of horror. "You're not going to back me." He glared at Kade. "What did Mia say to ruin it?"

Wow, nothing like throwing your partner under the bus. "She's been great," Kade answered, trying to size up the situation. "In fact, I like that you're a team. Why would you blame her?"

"I didn't mean it. Things pop out of my mouth when I'm nervous." Jordan sprung from the floor. "Mia and I are besties."

"You never told me about her," Kade said in a stern tone. He suddenly saw Jordan in a different light. *What other lies has he told? He's desperate. In a way I can't blame him, but desperation makes you do weird things.*

Jordan hung his head. "I thought you were looking for a single designer. Once you saw our work, I'd hoped you'd change your mind. Then I'd introduce Mia." He put his arm around her. "Sorry."

"It's okay. Kade knows everything now. He didn't run screaming from the deli when he discovered the truth."

"Hey, speaking of food. Your order came."

Mia shook her head. "A little late. I'll put it in the fridge."

"Already done," Jordan answered. "Now let's get back to this unpleasant news."

Kade cleared his throat. "I only have a certain amount of time and money to dedicate to this project. After many inquiries into fashion week, someone gave me a great proposal. If I could fill a spot in the new designer category this summer, I'd get a guaranteed spot in the spring fashion week show next year."

"Isn't the new and up-and-coming designer show held somewhere else? As they say, 'Off-off Broadway'?" Jordan asked.

"Yes, it is. Take it or leave it. I've just handed you the opportunity of a lifetime." Kade paused, giving time for his words to sink in. "I know it's short notice but between the two of you, can you come up with a portfolio? It doesn't need to be a full collection."

"Yes," Mia said, stepping forward. "We can do it. We are grateful for the opportunity."

"You two probably want to talk," Kade said, looking longingly at Mia. "I'll just…" He jutted his thumb over his shoulder.

"Thanks again," Mia said, not moving.

Walk me to the door. Act like you forgive me. This couldn't have gone any worse. Was it my presentation? I suck at this. Smith! I'm coming for you. Kade headed for the door. "I'll check in tomorrow."

* * * *

The door shut gently behind Kade, and Mia held her breath until she was sure he left. Anger welled up inside her. "Jordan!" she yelled, wanting to shake him. "What is going on?"

He covered his face with both hands. "I didn't want to blow it, Mee! I was scared." He dropped his arms to his sides. "Forgive me?"

Mia took a cleansing breath. "Give me time. I can't stay mad at you because we need to work on a spring/summer line *now*. As in, no dinner until we come up with a plan."

"Didn't you already start something?" Jordan crumpled his face into a plea for help.

"They're just doodles."

"You never doodle. Let me be the judge."

"Fine. You get waters from the fridge and join me at my desk," Mia answered.

"Oh! With all the drama, I almost forgot! Guess who I saw in Washington Square?"

"I have no idea," Mia shouted, although the kitchen was steps away.

"Mason Andrews! Do you believe it?"

"Mason from design school? He's here in New York?"

"Yes," Jordan said as he returned and placed a water bottle in her cup holder. "This shouldn't be hard. Guess why?"

"No!"

"Yes." Jordan nodded. "We have competition. Mason applied to the 'Off Broadway' show and got accepted. He's living here now."

"He's good." Mia cracked the cap on the bottle.

"Never a fan," Jordan said with a wave of the hand.

"Stop it. He wasn't nice to us because he viewed us as his major competition," Mia said. "Surely he's matured by now."

"No. If anything, he's taken a backward slide." Jordan made a face.

"Enough about Mason. Let's discuss color." Mia tapped her chin. "Coral pink. Navy blazer. Bright white."

"We were using plum in the winter collection, what about grape for summer?"

"It's a start. I'm drawn to pistachio and rose, too." Mia grabbed her chalks and made swirls across a page. "I reminded Kade he needed to find models as soon as possible."

"Good luck to him." Jordan raked a hand through his hair. "Why did this happen to us? I'm not good at working fast and under pressure," he moaned.

"You're not helping. Sit." Mia gestured to the desk across from hers.

They worked in silence for an hour. Jordan stopped what he was doing and looked at Mia. "I didn't forget."

"Forget what?" Mia knitted her brow.

"This coming weekend. You're supposed to go home for your great-uncle's memorial service."

"Not anymore."

"You have to! You go every year."

"You said it. They have it every year. I can skip one."

"It's something you shouldn't miss." Jordan looked at her from the corner of his eye. "Isn't it some Japanese tradition to honor the dead?"

"You are referring to Obon, The Festival of the Dead. It's held in August, not July. This isn't the same thing," Mia corrected him. "When Great-uncle Kaito died, my grandmother, his sister, wanted to hold a memorial in his honor every year."

"So, no lanterns or small bonfires to guide him home?" Jordan asked.

"Yes, we still do that. And we float lanterns on the water to guide him back to the spirit world at the end of the weekend. It's a way to honor him."

"Why not wait a month? Do during Obon?"

"Because," Mia said with a sigh. "This is the month he died."

"Oh." Jordan went back to work but kept peeking up at her.

"What?" Mia asked.

"How many years?"

"This will be the fifth year."

"Oh, Mee, you have to go. It's the fifth anniversary."

"I told you. There will be more memorials. I can't risk leaving here. We need every waking moment to work."

"Okay." Jordan held up his hands. "I'm done trying to convince you but remember these are the things you can never get back. The fifth anniversary?" He lifted a shoulder. "Just saying."

* * * *

Kade walked through Washington Square Park to work off some of his repressed emotions. Not knowing who to call first, he wandered aimlessly until he ended up at the fountain. *Gabe? Maybe Beau. No! The wonderful Mr. Smith.* He found a park bench, took out his burner phone and hit the speed dial.

"Mr. Phillips, a wonderful day for a walk in the park," Smith said when he answered. "Although a bit of humidity in the air, isn't there?"

What? We're talking about weather? Wait. He knows where I am? "I'm checking in, Smith. I told Jordan and Mia there was a change in plans. They didn't take it well."

"Mia? I thought Jordan was the designer you'd chosen to help."

"He has a partner and conveniently left that part out. Don't know why."

"Interesting. Did he plan to leave her out completely?"

"I can't say. Mia told me he's her best friend."

"But is he?"

"Is that my mission? To solve the mystery of Mia and Jordan? Are they best friends or not? Sounds like a soap opera instead of a mission," Kate said in a sarcastic tone.

"Of course not," Smith answered. "Are they both on board with the date change?"

"From what I could tell, Mia handled it better than Jordan. He got stressed out."

"Opposite personalities? Yin and yang?"

"Perhaps." Kade did not want to discuss Mia. He found her interesting and beautiful. They got along well until he dropped the fashion bomb. Any designer would balk at the demand. Yet something changed. Her demeanor, the way she treated him. "Will I discover the mission this week?"

"If I may be frank, Mr. Phillips, your mission is not set in stone like the others. Something may happen. Or it may not. Yet it is the most important assignment of all."

"Okay, now *that* makes sense." Kade wanted to throw the phone as far as he could. "How do I get the guys' money back if it, whatever *it* is, doesn't happen?"

"All things come to those who wait," Smith replied.

"Hold on there, Smith. I heard you were the master at yanking us around, but this is ridiculous." Kade took a breath. "Smith?" He waited for a response.

"Damn! He hung up on me!" Kade hopped from the bench, walked to the street entrance of the park and hailed a cab to take him back to the loft in Soho. "What do I do now? Oh! I know. Wait."

CHAPTER THREE

"It's eight o'clock already. We should eat," Mia said, sliding from her stool. "I want to change before we go out."

"To a bar?" Jordan had perked up when she'd called time.

"I said eat, Jordan." Mia started down the short hall to her bedroom and paused. *That's funny. I thought I shut this door.* She could see through a small space between door and frame. *This old crappy building. It probably popped open. I'm sure it's done it before.*

When she pushed open the door, Mia found the room exactly as she'd left it. Dropping to the floor, she piled up her treasures and returned them to the carryon, zipped it shut and rolled it into the closet. While there, she pulled a cotton dress from a hangar, removed her t-shirt and shorts and tossed them into a laundry bag. She'd love a shower after working so long in the warm apartment, but it had to wait. *I'll just get sweaty in the bar.*

Mia found Jordan changed and waiting at the door. Her heart did a little flip. He looked so handsome in a crisp, white shirt and black cotton pants. Slipping on her black sandals that she always left by the front door, Mia looked over at Jordan. "Ready."

"I will compromise." Jordan smiled. "A restaurant with a good bar."

"Deal."

The evening air felt muggy and clung to her skin. July's humidity had been horrible, worse than Mia recalled. When Jordan opened the door to the restaurant, a cool blast of air and fried food hit them. It was a casual establishment where one placed their order, then found a seat.

"I'll get drinks. You order," Jordan said, putting a hand on her back. "You know what I want. White wine for you?"

"Make it a fizzy white."

"Ooh, look at you. Bold and daring." Jordan teased.

"Don't stay too long in the bar," Mia scolded.

"Me?" Jordan widened his eyes. "Never."

"Right." Mia laughed. "Someone will start a conversation with you, then fifteen minutes later you'll be like, Oh! Mia's waiting." She watched Jordan head to the bar area, got in line and ordered two veggie burgers. She and Jordan weren't completely vegan, but tried to eat healthy, especially with the hours they kept. She pictured them working once they returned home, even if it was two in the morning.

After she ordered, Mia took her number and searched for a table. She plopped the stand in the middle of one against a side wall. When she was about to sit, she heard a voice from the past.

"Mia Takeda? The queen bee of design school?"

Mia turned to face the person who'd called to her. She hadn't seen her since graduation almost eight years ago. "Poppy?"

"Yes, it's me!" Poppy held out her arms with a huge grin on her face. "I can't believe it! It's so good to see you."

Poppy Regal looked the part of a fashion designer. Animal print skin-tight dress, four-inch heels and over the top makeup. Heavy black liner and false eyelashes framed her chocolate eyes. She'd dyed her honey blonde hair platinum and wore it in a high ponytail. A jeweled clip at least three inches tall was wrapped around the base.

Mia always thought Poppy was an exotic beauty with her slightly hooked nose and cat-like eyes. Her name did not fit her look. But Poppy's parents had done her a favor. They'd given her a great name for a designer.

After they hugged, Mia asked, "Is there a Poppy Brand yet?"

"Soon, I hope," Poppy squealed. "I'm using my full name though. I thought it sounds cool." She struck a pose. "Poppy Regal."

"It does. I always thought so." Mia smiled at the one person besides Jordan, she considered a good friend from school.

Mia and Poppy had gravitated toward each other the first year at design school. With Poppy's outgoing personality and good looks and Mia feeling shy and younger than the rest, they were a good fit. As the year went on, Jordan had become part of their group and by their third year he had taken over her life. She and Poppy drifted apart.

"Why are you in New York?" Mia asked.

"Looking for a place to live," Poppy answered.

"Really? Jordan ran into Mason Andrews today. He recently moved here."

Poppy made a face. "Mason 'I can do anything better than you' Andrews?" She licked her red lips. "Although he's correct about some things."

"Poppy! Did you sleep with him? I thought you were mortal enemies."

"Haven't you heard the saying 'keep your enemies close'?" Poppy giggled. "Well, it only happened a few times." She shook her head. "No, make that whenever I needed a good lay. What about you? Boyfriend?" She pointed at Mia. "Don't tell me you're still with Jordan?

He's so controlling. Will he even let you have a boyfriend?"

"Um, yeah, he would. We moved here three years ago. We have an apartment in the Village."

"You need to get out from under his grip, both professionally and personally," Poppy said, putting a hand to the side of her mouth as if telling a secret. "You could go solo. We used to call you the queen bee of designs."

"Stop." Mia felt the heat travel up to her cheeks.

"Come on! You're not twenty anymore, Mia. You must be at least twenty-eight by now. Am I right?"

"Yes."

"A *woman* with a mind of her own. Don't let Jordan hold you back."

"Did I hear my name?" Jordan balanced two drinks in his hands as he made his way through the growing crowd. He set them on the table, then did a double take. "Poppy Regal?"

"Jordan!" Poppy yelled as if she'd gotten the best present ever.

"Whatever are you doing here, girl? Look at you. Love the print."

Mia never understood how people could switch from gossiping about a person to acting like their best friend when they saw them.

"Did you hear, Mee?" Jordan nudged. "Poppy applied and got accepted into the new designer show. Gosh, they let anyone in." He teased Poppy and they laughed, while he rolled his eyes so only Mia saw.

"Stop!" Poppy placed her hand on her stomach to subdue the laughter. "I'm sure you're beyond applying for grants and praying to get into small shows like this to get noticed."

"Oh, no, Pops," Jordan replied. "We'll be there, too."

Poppy's jaw dropped. Mia felt the urge to place a finger under her chin and close it for her. Instead, she said, "We just found out."

Jordan shot her a look as if to say "quiet".

"Really? Maybe they chose you last minute because someone dropped out. I've known since March! Or was it before that? Anyway, I'm sure between the two of you, you'll pull something marvelous together. Have you picked a color scheme?" Poppy lifted her brows.

"Now, Poppy," Jordan said. "We don't share company secrets."

"Of course! Just teasing." Poppy scanned the room. "Ooh, look who walked in. Mason Andrews. I'll make him nervous and say hello. *Ciao*, for now."

"You do that, Pops," Jordan called as she walked away, then turned to Mia. "Looks like our burgers are coming."

Mia and Jordan took a seat and thanked the server for bringing their food. "Who else are we going to see?" Jordan asked. "Did the entire class apply to the show?"

"Don't be surprised if there are more people we know. Our school was one of the best. Poppy and Mason are good. They deserve to be here," Mia said, examining her burger to see where to make the first bite. "How did you know she was in the show?"

"Mason. He was in the bar."

"He knew?"

"Obviously."

"I thought he just walked in."

"He went out for a smoke." Jordan smirked. "Idiot."

"So, those two are still in contact or ran into each other here. Poppy acted like she didn't know Mason was in New York."

"She's sneaky as the day is long," Jordan said.

Mia wrinkled her nose. "Did you make that up?"

"Maybe." Jordan lifted a shoulder. "All I know is the stakes just got higher."

* * * *

"How can I keep this from Chase? He'll kill me if I ask his sister to come to New York. His whole family is against her modeling." Kade rubbed his chin as he talked to himself in the bathroom mirror. "Which isn't fair. On the other hand, she may agree not to tell him. But I need his plane to get her here fast." He chuckled. "If I don't stop talking to myself and call Ella, I won't know if any of this will work."

Chase's sister was twenty-two, had graduated college this year and was ready to make her mark in the world. She wanted to be a model but her parents, Chase's mom and stepdad, had insisted on four years at a university before she ventured out into the world. Kade could now help with her big break. She was getting a late start so she'd need help, but not much. Slender and tall at five feet nine, her copper hair and dark blue eyes would make her a standout.

"Kade!" Ella squealed when she heard his voice. "It's been ages."

"How are you, Ella?"

"Ooh, so formal. I'm great, and you?"

"Same. Look, I'll get right to the point. I need your help." Without giving too much away, Kade explained how he needed models for the show. "Any agency will tell me most of their models have bookings or wouldn't want to walk this show. No offense."

"None taken. Gives me the advantage."

"Am I asking too much? Can you find more models?"

"Fall fashion week is always the beginning of September, right? It gives me barely six weeks to round up some of my friends and working models I know, but it's doable."

"You can help me with more models? That's great! And Ella, this show is in August." Kade cringed. "You've got less time."

"Oh." Ella paused. "That's fine. Most of us are catalog models looking for a break. So yes. I can fly into New York whenever you want. It's better if we plan this together."

"When's best for you?" Kade couldn't believe his good fortune. If Ella helped him with this side of the show, he could focus on his mission. The one that may or may not happen.

"Is Monday okay? Should I call Chase and arrange a flight?"

"Will he let you come?" Kade asked. *Why am I afraid of the guy? He's my friend. He'll figure out why I need her.*

"He's not the boss of me," Ella laughed.

"Make sure you tell him you're doing it for me," Kade added, hoping Chase would realize this was part of his mission.

"I'll text you the details when I have them," Ella answered. "And thanks for believing in me, Kade."

"Always." Once he ended the call, Kade's thoughts went to Mia. He had no way of contacting her, never asking for her number. Phone still in hand, he pressed Jordan's number.

"Jordan here."

"Jordan, it's Kade."

"Hello, Captain. Enjoying your evening?"

Kade picked up on background noise and determined Jordan wasn't at home. "It's all right. Are you with Mia by any chance?"

"Yeah, we're having veggie burgers at Town Hall. We'll probably hang out here for a while."

"May I speak with her?"

"Sure."

It took longer than Kade thought it should, but Mia finally came online. "Kade?"

"Mia, I never got your number. I didn't want to ask Jordan for it. I thought you should give it to me."

"For business purposes?"

"That … and more. Look, Mia, I thought we had a connection. Then I said something stupid and blew it."

"You said nothing stupid. I felt overwhelmed by all I found out today."

"Then we're good?"

"Yes."

Kade heard her let out a small breath of air and wished to be there in person. *What have you done to me, Mia Takeda!* "Have a good night. I'm sorry if I interrupted your dinner."

"You didn't," Mia replied. "I'll get your number from Jordan and text you."

"Great. I'll wait to hear from you." Kade wanted to punch himself in the face. *I never have trouble talking to people. Doesn't Gabe call me 'Magnet' because people are drawn to me? The one I want to notice me is holding me at arm's length. There must be more to it. And I plan to find out.*

* * * *

"Was that so hard?" Jordan asked, sticking out his lower lip. "What did the guy do to you at lunch?"

"Nothing!" Mia would never admit she was attracted to their mentor. It could ruin their business relationship. Plus, if Kade ever discovered Mia could foot the bill for the show and those to come, he may feel deceived. Not the best way to start a romance. *Romance! What am I thinking? Best if I keep my distance.*

Mia felt a tap on her shoulder. She glanced up to find Poppy and Mason standing behind her. "Hey, Mia," Poppy said. "I forgot to ask for your number. We must get together now that I will live here."

"Here? As in Greenwich Village?" Mia asked, then realized she sounded disappointed. "Sure. There's a lot of places I can take you," she answered in a perky voice as they exchanged phones. Mia looked up after placing her number in Poppy's phone list and made eye contact with Mason. "Hey, Mason. Haven't seen you in a while."

"Same." Mason crossed his arms. Dark, smoldering good looks, smoky eyes and a few days' growth of beard made him irresistible to some.

Why do I always notice the eyes? "Congrats on making the show."

Mason lifted a shoulder. "From what I hear, anyone can get in."

"I highly doubt that," Mia replied, returning Poppy's phone, her number now in the contacts list.

"There will be plenty of competition," Mason stated. "We want to get noticed. That's the point of the show."

"We're almost done here," Jordan interrupted and pointed to the plates on the table. "Why don't we meet you in the bar?" He gestured toward the U-shape bar through the wide opening which connected bar to restaurant.

"Come on, Mason." Poppy slid her arm through his. "I'm buying."

"Why didn't you say so earlier?" Mason's face brightened.

Mia watched them walk toward the bar, feeling they were far enough away that she could talk. "Jordan, why didn't you say anything?"

"I did. I said we needed to finish eating."

"Not that." Mia huffed. "In defense of the show. Or that not everyone gets a spot."

"Because I feel he's right. It's amateur hour. You only go, hoping someone will notice you. Besides, we have nothing to worry about. We'll blow Poppy *and* Mason out of the water."

"Maybe that's what he's afraid of," Mia said and leaned closer to Jordan. "I never trusted him. Don't tell him anything about our designs."

"I won't! I wouldn't. Mee, why would you say that?"

"You're swayed by a pretty face. He knows how to use you."

"Not and not," Jordan said with a laugh, then pushed back his chair. "Ready?"

"Yes, but let's not stay long." Mia joined him on the walk to the bar. "I want to go back to the apartment and work."

"You've heard the saying, Mee, all work and no play…"

"Makes Mia a dull girl?" Mia finished for him. Before she could counter with her own dig, her eyes locked with a man on the other side of the bar. "Oh. No," she whispered.

CHAPTER FOUR

Rafe Salvadore. He stared at Mia with his ice-blue eyes. Ones which used to send a carnal sensation straight to her female parts but now gave her the chills. He lifted and dropped his brows quickly, never breaking eye contact.

Does he think that will make me run to him? No way in hell. Is he trying to send me a sensual smile?

The best smiles started in the eyes and spread to the mouth. Rafe's smile never reached his eyes. It reminded her more of a sneer. *What is he up to?* Mia dug her nails into Jordan's upper arm.

"Ow!" Jordan pulled away. He looked at her and followed her gaze. "Oh, hell no. He's back? Don't you dare go over there. Pompous ass. Standing there holding a beer in one hand and beckoning you over with his sexy blue eyes."

"I wouldn't. Never." Mia shook her head. Her stomach danced. The sandwich now felt like a stone at the bottom. "I thought he left the city. I haven't seen him since the end of March."

"Do you know what he does for a living? Didn't he give you some bullshit about having to travel for work? He's probably got a wife and three kids in every state."

"Jordan," Mia hissed. "He's coming around the bar."

"Quick. Hide."

"What?" Mia grabbed Jordan by the arm and marched him to the bar. "Order us a drink while I keep an eye out for him."

Before she had a chance to get her bearings she heard, "Mia Takeda. It is so good to see you again."

At six four, Rafe towered over her. She'd always liked tall men with dark hair and interesting eyes. When they first met, Rafe filled the qualifications and once she got to know him, admired his strong personality. He never took "no" for an answer when he wanted something.

"Hi, Rafe," Mia said. "I haven't seen you in months."

"Yeah, sorry about that. I got called out of town. Business." Rafe held out his arms, beer bottle still in one hand. "But now I'm back."

"I see."

Rafe took a step closer. "Miss me?"

The bar swarmed with people and Mia had nowhere to go. "Not really."

"Not really?" Rafe bent down to whisper in her ear. "Not even the sex?"

Mia cringed, hoping Jordan would come to her rescue.

"There you are," a familiar voice said. "Sorry I'm late." Kade stepped into view, acting as if he belonged there.

"Kade?" Mia blinked, not believing he truly was there.

"Yeah, it's me. You told me to meet you here, right?" He winked, sending a silent message that he was in on the game. His amber eyes twinkled mischievously.

"Right. We have business to discuss," Mia answered.

"And you promised me a drink," Kade teased. He turned to Rafe. "Kade Phillips. And you are?"

"Mia's boyfriend."

Kade didn't flinch. "In all the time I've known her, she's never mentioned a boyfriend."

Like one whole day. I love it. "He's an *ex*, Kade. He came over to say hi."

"In that case, are you done here, Mia?"

"Definitely. Jordan's over there. Let's join him."

"We're not finished, Mia. I'll call you," Rafe exclaimed as he walked away.

"You okay?" Kade whispered. "You had that deer in the headlights look."

"I did?" *Damn, girl!* Mia scolded herself. "I can handle him. My boss doesn't need to rescue me."

"Is that how you see me?" Kade's smile seemed sad. "As your boss?"

"Yes … I have to … it's best…"

"Now I understand the cold shoulder."

"I didn't…"

"You did." Kade pointed farther down the bar. "Seems Jordan got away from you."

* * * *

When Kade saw Rafe hovering over Mia as if he owned her, his blood boiled. He'd known guys like that his whole life. They worked out at the gym, wore the latest fashion and a shadow of a beard. It appealed to some women. Yet, it surprised him that Mia had fallen for his act. But after a few seconds of speaking with Rafe, he'd seen why. The guy was forceful, making Kade instantly dislike him.

Kade swore Mia was still trembling and wished he could pull her into his arms. He longed to tell her things were okay. "Don't let him get to you. Let him assume I'm your boyfriend," he said to the back of her head as they walked toward Jordan.

With that, Mia spun on her heels and planted a kiss on his lips. Kade went weak in the knees with shock and desire. Her lips tasted of sugar and wine and he wanted more. When she stepped back, he asked, "Did he see?"

"Maybe. He's looking now."

Kade brought her to him and placed a slow, lingering kiss on her pink petal lips. She tightened against him, then relaxed, melting into his body. "Hey," he whispered. "You okay?"

"I will be. Thanks for pretending to be my boyfriend. You can stop now. Rafe left the bar."

"Do you want me to stop?"

Mia looked at him from under her long lashes. "No," she whispered. "But we have work to do."

"That kiss looked hot!" Jordan shoved a drink in Mia's hand and patted Kade on the back. "Congrats, Captain. She's a great gal."

"Gal?" Mia stared daggers at him. "This is not the nineteen fifties. Although you *are* obsessed with the fashion from the era. If you want to know, Kade was helping me out. Pretending to be my boyfriend."

"If that's pretending?" Jordan fanned himself with his hand. "I want some of that."

"Please stop," Mia said under her breath, but Kade heard and gave her a wink.

"Did you two make any progress today?" Kade asked, hoping the change in subject would help.

"A baby step," Jordan replied. "We are in agreement over color and style."

"Did you find any models?" Mia questioned Kade.

"I believe I have. She'll be here Monday to help me find more. I'll let Ella oversee that side of things, freeing me up for other work."

"Ella?" Jordan raised his brows. "You must know her pretty well if she agreed so quickly."

Kade nodded. "She's a friend."

"A model *friend*." Jordan wiggled his brows. "You two ever hook up?"

"Jordan!" Mia poked him.

"No, I'm actually friends with her brother and he'd kill me if I ever came near his little sister." Kade chuckled. Being in the industry, he associated with many designers and models. He could get some well-known names to assist him in an instant. Yet, if Jordan had no clue how well connected Kade was, he wanted to keep it that way. "While I have you two together, let's discuss patterns. How soon can you get your drawings to me? Say, next week? The loft is ready to go. I hired dressmakers and pattern cutters. There's plenty of room for them, and you, to work. I take up only a small part of the space."

"You're living there?" Mia asked.

"Yeah, you've got to come and see the place."

"Where?"

"Soho."

"Ooh," Jordan cried. "We hit the jackpot. Our mentor is moving us to Soho."

"It sounds nice," Mia said, giving Jordan an elbow to his ribs. "Don't mind him. He's always like this."

"I don't mind at all," Kade said with a smile.

"Jordan!" Poppy called. "Help me settle a bet."

"You know her?" Kade bobbed his head in Poppy's direction.

"That's Poppy Regal, and yes, it's her real name," Mia answered. "The guy she's with is Mason Andrews. We went to design school with them. They've moved here." She took a breath. "They're in the showcase too."

"Are they competition?"

"Yes, they're good. Poppy might be better than Mason."

"Then let's get you over to the loft so you can see the setup. The sooner you get started, the better. I'll text you the address. In fact, how about dinner at my place tomorrow? And don't worry about getting a car, I'll have someone pick you up."

"Sounds great. What about Jordan? When will he see the loft?"

"He can come over Thursday. The next two days, I want you all to myself."

* * * *

"Not fair. You get to see the loft before I do." Jordan followed Mia around the apartment as she got ready for her date. "And he's sending a car for you."

"It's not business. We're having dinner so we can get to know each other. Besides, we're both going on Thursday, so we better have something to show him." Mia pointed at him. "Keep working while I'm gone. I promise I won't stay long."

"Fine." Jordan walked over to his desk. "I'll color while you're gone."

"You sound like you're five years old." Mia giggled. "Why don't you go out to dinner? Treat yourself. Then come back and work."

"Maybe."

"Don't do this, Jordan."

"What? I'm not doing anything."

"Every time I have a date, you give me a hard time."

"I'm not."

"You are." Mia planted her hands on her hips. "I don't do that to you." She waited for a response and got nothing. "I love you, bestie."

"I love you, too," Jordan mumbled.

Mia's phone buzzed. The car service had arrived. "I promise to be home before midnight."

"Okay, Cinderella, have fun," Jordan said with a wave.

"Or earlier!" Mia called as she shut the front door.

Excitement speed through her body. She couldn't wait to go to the loft and have dinner at Kade's without interruption. Hundreds of questions ran through her mind. Mia swallowed. *He may have questions for me.* She placed her hand below her throat and took a calming breath. When she reached street level, she gasped at what she saw. A limo driver, dressed in uniform, stood next to a black Mercedes.

No, that can't be for me. When Kade said he'd send a car service, I didn't expect this. Mia opened the apartment door, and the man rushed forward.

"Mia Takeda?"

"Yes?"

"I am here to drive you to Mr. Phillips' home." He opened the passenger side back door.

"Why, thank you." Mia slipped inside, landing on a buttery soft leather seat.

Mia straightened and smoothed her skirt over her knees. She'd chosen a sleeveless black and white floral maxi dress with a split up past her knee. A great find from one of the more expensive stores "off the rack" collection. It had some stretch for a smooth fit, showing off her curves. She leaned against the seat and watched out the window as they drove to Soho. *May as well enjoy the ride.*

The driver pulled up in front of a building which appeared to be in the middle of renovations. It had "Units Available" in the front window. "Mr. Phillips' apartment is on the top floor," he announced over his shoulder. "I'll let him know we've arrived. If you'll wait, I'll come around to help you out."

Mia cocked her head to see better and glanced up, quickly counting eight floors. "Greene Street," she said under her breath. She'd shopped in Soho many times in her teens with Grandmother Takeda and her mother. They'd call a "Girls' Weekend", board the family jet and fly to New York City whenever the mood struck them. Grandmother insisted on staying at the Plaza near Central Park while there.

The car door opened, and the driver offered Mia his hand. "Mr. Phillips is coming down to greet you."

Mia took his hand and stepped out into the familiar surroundings. Some of her favorite shops and boutiques were still there. She tried to look overwhelmed and impressed as any first-time visitor to the street would.

"Mia!" Kade opened the door as she approached.

"Hello, Kade." Mia bit into her lip to keep from gasping at the sight of him. Tall, lean and muscular, he'd rolled the arms of his white linen shirt to below the elbow. He wore khaki color linen pants and casual sandals. When he leaned in to greet her, he smelled as if he'd stepped from the shower, all clean and spicy. His layered curls still had a few wet strands, making him look even more attractive.

"You look beautiful," Kade whispered into her ear. "Follow me." He gestured toward the elevator.

They stepped off at the eighth floor into a small foyer. The loft ran from the front of the building to the back. Enormous, arched windows built into the front wall let in natural light. Black walnut hardwood floors were a good contrast to the white walls. The outer wall of exposed brick, opposite of where they stood, gave the feel of modern and vintage all in one.

Kade pointed to the area in front of the windows filled with long tables, sewing machines and huge design tables. "This is where you'll work." He nodded the other way. "And have use of a kitchen, seating and dining area."

The color scheme ran from brown to natural tones. Mia especially liked the brown and cream buffalo checked high back settee. A wall with a single door ran behind the gleaming stainless-steel kitchen dividing the space. She guessed Kade's master suite was behind it.

"Well." Kade shrugged. "Do you like the place?"

"It's wonderful. What a great place to work." Mia glanced toward the closed-off area. "And play."

"I'm glad you like it." Kade smiled. "I did something I rarely do. I liked the building so much I bought it."

Real estate? Good call. "I'm impressed," Mia said. "Why the entire building?"

"Investment. Plus, I wanted control of the place." Kade rubbed his chin. "I don't really know why. I usually lease places to live and for work. Makes life easier."

"Then you have no roots," Mia said in a sad voice. She'd read between the lines. Kade hadn't found himself yet, much like her. They had more in common than she realized.

"I lease apartments around the world. Tokyo and Paris, for example. I want to have somewhere familiar to stay when I travel. When I go home to Colorado, I live with my friend Gabe in Boulder. I consider his place home."

"He's a great friend," Mia said. "You knew each other before you made your money. Those are the best kind of friends to have."

"We think so." Kade placed his hand on Mia's back. "May I offer you a glass of wine? I noticed you drank white last night, but what is your preference?"

"White is fine. Whatever you have."

"Then you must choose." Kade escorted her to the wine fridge. "I ordered in some wines from Napa Valley since you said you were from California. Any favorites?"

Favorite? I could tick off the wineries I've visited and my preferences. "Let me see." Mia pretended to study the choices, then touched a bottle of white with a familiar label. "This is fine."

Kade slipped the bottle from its place and twirled it in his hand. "I'll get this open and we can sit over there." He tilted his head toward the living room. "If you don't mind, there's a charcuterie board in the fridge?"

"Not at all," Mia answered, opening the door to find a wooden platter filled with cured meats, cheeses, nuts, dried fruit, and jam. "Crackers?"

"In the basket," Kade said with a nod toward the counter. He popped out the cork and poured the wine.

"This is wonderful," Mia said, placing the food on a table in front of the loveseat she'd admired.

"I ordered dinner to come in two hours. I hope you like keto fried chicken, sweet potato fries and Brussel sprouts." Kade took a sip of wine and put his stemmed glass on the table. "I've been thinking about what you said."

Mia wrinkled her brow and stared at him. "Refresh my memory."

"About us."

"Oh," she acknowledged.

"You're right. We need to focus on work, not a relationship."

CHAPTER FIVE

Her stomach twisted, and Mia's heart stopped for a second.

"I want to date you, get to know you," Kade continued. "We can do the 'get to know you' part now, but you don't need other distractions like a pretend boyfriend." He chuckled. "Although I'd like to drop the pretend."

"I would like that, too." Mia lowered her eyes. Everything he said made sense, yet why was she disappointed?

"You seem … sad?" Kade voice held a touch of concern. "Did I say something wrong?'

"No, you said everything right." Mia leaned toward him and left a kiss on his lips. "I still want to do this."

"Your wish is my command," Kade said and returned a longer, deeper kiss.

Mia longed to get lost in the moment. Yet her head won the battle over her heart. Even though she was falling fast and furiously, she needed time. "Kade," she whispered. "I don't know if…"

"We can wait?" Kade teased.

How did he read my mind?

He leaned against the back of the sofa and ran his finger along her cheek. "This should put a damper on our feelings. I'll start the interview. Do you have any brothers or sisters?"

Caught off guard, Mia giggled. "Wow, you changed the subject fast! And no, I'm an only child. You?"

"One brother. Kristopher. He's two years younger."

"Hmm, he may be closer to my age," Mia joked.

Kade covered his heart and feigned hurt. "Tell me you like older men."

Mia closed one eye. "How much older?"

"Thirty?"

"Perfect." Mia slipped her hand into his.

"We do fit perfectly together, don't we?" Kade winked as he checked his phone. "Food's here."

While Kade retrieved their dinner, Mia looked at her cell. It was almost nine pm. She sent a text to Jordan telling him not to work too hard. After a minute and no response, she slipped her phone back into her bag, deciding to enjoy the evening and not worry about her partner.

"Join me at the table?" Kade asked.

Impressed that he'd set the dining table before she arrived, Mia admired the simplistic sand color plates speckled with brown and champagne-colored flatware. They plated their food and Kade poured more wine. "Do you have plans tomorrow night?" he asked.

Mia shook her head, not wanting to answer with a mouthful of food.

"This has been so relaxing for me. I'd like to do it again."

Mia studied him closely, noticing for the first time the rings under his eyes, the worry on his face. She swallowed and said, "Only if you let me bring the food."

"Deal."

"And tell me what's on your mind. It can't just be the show."

"Oh! Speaking of the show…" Kade squirmed in his seat. "It's not in September as we originally thought. It's scheduled for the last weekend of August. I double checked the date before calling Ella Rivers."

Mia pulled her brows together. "Who?"

"The model who will help with the show."

"Oh, right. This gives us even less time."

The evening seemed to fly by as she and Kade compared childhoods and discussed the show. Mia checked her fit band. It was after eleven pm. "I don't mean to cut the night short…" She gave Kade soulful eyes.

"I understand. I'll call the car."

Mia gathered her things and glanced around the loft. "It's perfect," she said under her breath. She joined Kade at the elevator and they rode in silence to the first floor.

Before going out to the street, Kade tugged on her hand. "A goodnight kiss?"

Mia leaned into him and lifted her face as he came closer. Their lips met, and a shiver went through her. "I'll see you tomorrow. Same time?" she asked.

"Yes," Kade answered, guiding Mia from the elevator. They went outside to the waiting car. "Stay safe," he whispered and kissed her on the cheek.

The driver wove his way through lower Manhattan making his way to Greenwich Village. Mia stared out the window, reflecting on the evening. Kade was a gentleman for sure. She'd sent signals to the contrary, but he'd respected the fact she needed to concentrate on work. *Why doesn't he have a girlfriend?* Mia smiled. *Although I'm glad he doesn't.*

When the car pulled up to her building, Mia checked the time. *Eleven thirty. Home before midnight, as promised.* "Don't get out, Damien. I'm fine." She'd made a point to learn the driver's name in case he picked her up again. "Are you part of Kade's staff?" she asked as she reached for the door handle.

"Yes, I am," Damien replied with a smile.

"I'd still like to give you something for driving me all over the city," Mia said.

"Oh, no, Mr. Phillips takes good care of me. When he's not in town I work for his friend, Beau Miller."

Interesting. "Well, thank you. I'll see you tomorrow?"

"You can count on it. Same time?"

"Yes," she answered.

As Mia slid from the car something caught her eye. A tall figure stood in the shadows of her building. She opened her handbag and dug through until she found what she needed. Pepper spray in one hand, apartment key in the other, she started for the door.

"Mia!" Rafe stepped into the light.

"Rafe, you scared me." Mia placed her hand over her heart, keys jangling. "What are you doing here so late?"

"Late? This is early for a city that doesn't sleep." Rafe chuckled as he came closer.

Mia sucked in a breath. She wanted to yell, "Stay where you are," yet nothing came out.

"I rang your bell, but no one answered. I gave it fifteen minutes to see if you'd come home."

"Jordan didn't answer?" Mia wrinkled her brow.

"No, he didn't. Do you mind if I come up? I'd like to talk."

"Um." Mia bite into her bottom lip. "I'm pretty busy right now, Rafe."

"Ms. Takeda?" Damien's voice broke into their conversation. "Is everything all right?"

Grateful for the save, Mia turned to him. "Yes, I'm fine. Could you wait until I'm inside?"

"Sure." Damien gave a nod.

"Goodnight, Rafe," Mia said as she passed him on the way to the entrance.

Rafe took her by arm. "Mia, come on. We need to talk. I'm sorry I disappeared without a text or a call. I wouldn't have left, but it was important. Let me explain."

"Sir, you need to take your hands off her." Damien now stood next to them. Seeing him up close, Mia was certain he worked out daily and thought he could easily get a job as a bodyguard.

Rafe held his hands in the air. "We're friends. We know each other."

"Is that true, Ms. Takeda?"

"Yes, Damien. Exes. I haven't seen him in a while."

"Let me walk you to your door." Damien tilted his head toward the building and waited until Mia got inside.

What the hell just happened? Why is Rafe showing up after all these months? Mia pounded up the stairs to the third floor. She unlocked the door to find the apartment dark. "Jordan?" She turned on the lights and walked to his drafting table. *No recent work.* "I'm going to bed."

Mia flopped onto her mattress with a little bounce and gazed at the ceiling. Her head spun, trying to make sense of what happened. "Who cares? Hopefully Rafe got the message." She wanted to crawl in bed and dream of Kade. Pulling her body up from the soft mattress, she sat on the edge. Facing her closet, Mia stared at her clothes neatly aligned on hangers, the door slid all the way back. "I never leave the door open. Or did I just forget?" She grabbed a tank and shorts from a hook before sliding the door shut, slipped into her pajamas and set her ceiling fan on the highest speed.

Not sure if she could fall asleep, Mia sat close to the headboard, adjusted the pillows against her back and mindlessly swept through her phone.

* * * *

Kade returned to the loft, turned off the lights and sat in the moonlit room, staring out the front windows. He wanted to remember everything about Mia and their evening together, how she tasted, the scent of her perfume, the looks she gave him. He appreciated her intelligence and her sense of humor. She seemed to get him. Shaking his head, he chastised himself for being this caught up in a woman. He'd casually dated since high school, labeling no one as his girlfriend, although some considered him a boyfriend. His friend Gabe would say it was a fear of commitment and dating someone longer than a month might make the woman believe he was serious.

"What is the longest I ever dated someone?" Kade scratched the side of his chin. "Six months?" His phone pinged, drawing his attention away from thoughts of his dating life. "Damien?" He read the text and quickly called him.

"Yes, Mr. Phillips?"

"Damien, please for the hundredth time, call me Kade."

"Mr. Miller would not approve, sir."

"When you work for me, you don't answer to him," Kade stated.

"My brother would not agree."

Damien's brother, Wade, was Beau's sometimes driver and all-around man to get things done. Damien took Wade's place whenever his brother had a gig at a nightclub. Beau encouraged Wade's dream of becoming a musician, and Kade knew Beau got him jobs throughout the city. When not with Beau, Damien worked double-duty for Kade as a driver and bodyguard.

"Tell me what this guy looked like," Kade inquired.

"Tall, works out, dark hair, has one of those goatees that's barely there," Damien answered. "Should I continue?"

"No," Kade replied. "I have enough information. Thanks, Damien, you did the right thing. Are you available to pick up Mia same time tomorrow?"

"Definitely. Anything else?"

"No, have a good night."

As soon as Kade hung up, he called Mia.

"Kade?" She sounded breathless or maybe he woke her.

"I didn't…?"

"No, I couldn't sleep."

"Because of Rafe?"

He heard a gasp. "You know?"

"Damien texted me."

"I'm fine. Rafe got the message."

"Which was?"

"Leave me alone."

"I have two questions and I'll let you go. What is Rafe's last name?"

"Salvadore."

"Birthdate?"

"This sounds like an interrogation, Kade," Mia whispered.

"It's not. I have a friend who can look into his background."

"Now it really sounds like one." Mia paused. "We never got to birthdays. But I know he's your age. He'd brag he was an Aries, a powerful warrior."

"That helps. Thanks." Kade wanted to say something loving, comforting, yet felt it was too soon. "I'm looking forward to our dinner tomorrow."

"So am I. Is it all right if I ask Damien to take me somewhere beforehand?"

"Absolutely. Take care."

"You, too."

Kade waited until she hung up then dialed Beau, praying he'd be available. He didn't want to send the pyramid, the society's secret emoji, which meant someone wanted help or he needed a meeting with all six. He only wanted to talk to Beau.

"Kade?" Beau sounded wide awake when he answered.

"I need your help."

"Okay."

"Sorry. I should ask how you are, is Tess there and how's the business," Kade said, letting out a frustrated breath.

"All are fine, Kade. You sound concerned, as we all did when we were on our missions. How can I help?"

"I need all the information you can find on someone. I'll text you what I've got. And thanks, Beau. I mean it. You are the heart of the society. Everyone turns to you in their time of crisis."

"Because I own a security firm?" Beau joked.

"No, man, you give great advice … and own a security firm." Kade chuckled.

"Send me the info and hopefully I'll have a full dossier by the end of the week."

"Sounds good."

"I won't keep you, although I'd love to know how your assignment is going," Beau said.

"Worse than Gabe's. Smith told me I may or may not discover what it is."

"What? He is full of shit. It's almost like he's setting us up to lose."

"Agree, but I won't let him make fools of us. I'll solve this puzzle if it's the last thing I do."

"Don't say it like that." Beau chuckled nervously. "We're here for you. Call me anytime."

After ending the call, Kade dashed off what little information he had on Rafe Salvadore to Beau's phone. "I'll get to the bottom of this, you bastard. Why show up now after ghosting Mia for months?"

* * * *

Mia rolled out of bed, took a quick shower and went to the kitchen to start the coffeemaker. *If I make coffee, Jordan won't have an excuse to leave the apartment.* Checking the time, she'd hoped he'd appear by now. *Ten? I'm waking him up. He has an afternoon shift.* She walked down the short hall and knocked on his door.

"Go away," Jordan shouted.

"We need to work."

"Give me one more hour."

"No! Kade gave me some bad news last night," Mia called through the closed door. "The show is earlier than Fashion Week. We barely have a month to finish."

The door to Jordan's bedroom flew open. "What?"

His bloodshot eyes told the story. "Did you go out drinking last night?" Mia narrowed her eyes.

"Poppy and Mason called. I needed a break." Jordan rubbed the side of his head. "I have a killer hangover. I hope there's coffee."

"I made some." Mia stared at him. "Did you spill any secrets?"

"What? No! Or at least I don't think so. I barely remember the last hour."

"Jordan, so help me…!" Mia curled her fingers into fists.

"I'm kidding." Jordan placed an arm across her shoulders. "Let me grab a quick shower. I'll be out in five."

Mia scoured the cupboard for something to eat. She found a container of instant oatmeal and a package of pastry tarts. After making the oatmeal in the microwave, she divided it into two mugs and slid the pastries into the toaster.

"Mmm, love the smell of coffee in the morning," Jordan said, taking the two mugs of oatmeal to the table. "What the…? This is *not* coffee." He took his cup to the sink, turned on the disposal and washed it down the drain.

"Hey! I would have eaten it," Mia said as she poked him in the back.

Jordan poured coffee into the same mug and headed for the table. "How was the date?" he asked.

"We had a wonderful time. We're putting the dating thing on hold until you and I make some progress." Mia set her coffee on the table and placed her hands on her hips. "Which brings me to the question, why did you go out instead of working on designs?"

"I told you. They begged me." Jordan sipped from his mug. "They also like the name I chose for our design house. JorDan."

"The name makes it sound as if there's only one designer." Mia raised her brows.

"Yep, it does. They said after the show I should strike out on my own."

CHAPTER SIX

Mia fought back her emotions and fears all day. When she saw Kade, she burst into tears and almost dropped the carefully chosen sushi she'd brought as she slid from the backseat of the Mercedes. Kade rushed to her aid, took the box and ushered her up to the loft.

"What happened?" Kade put the food in his fridge and grabbed some tissues.

"Thanks." Mia sniffed, taking the tissue. "I don't know what came over me."

"Is it Rafe?"

Mia blinked and looked at Kade with wide eyes. "No. It's Jordan."

"What did he do?"

"Nothing. Never mind. It's over. We're fine."

"You don't appear fine," Kade said in a soft voice. "Come. Sit down. Why don't you tell me what happened, and I'll help you through it?"

"This morning…" Mia dabbed her eyes with the tissue and shook her head. "No, make that last night. Jordan wasn't home when I got in. He'd gone out, didn't leave a note. He never worked on our project. I couldn't find any new sketches or designs."

"I'm having my doubts about the man."

"No, please, don't." Mia placed her hand on Kade's arm. "When he's under pressure, Jordan needs to blow off steam. He does that from time to time. Disappears. Parties. Then he returns and is fine. Last night Jordan met Poppy and Mason and had too much to drink. He let them get into his head. They told him he should strike out on his own, especially since he had the coolest name for a designer."

"You're talking about Jor*dan*?" Kade asked.

"Yes, he's been trying it out on people to get their reaction."

"Are they stroking his ego to get information?" Kade asked.

"Maybe." Mia lifted a shoulder. "Jordan let the praise go to his head. He assured me it was just talk, and he'd never do what they suggested."

"From your tone, you sound like you don't believe him."

"There's something else." Mia twisted the tissue in her hands. "I'm not obsessive, but I like things organized and neat. I make my bed and close my closet door. Last night it was wide open."

"An honest mistake?"

"No," Mia said with a shake of the head. "I'm positive I closed it. I hate to even say this. It seems Jordan was snooping around my room after I left."

"Why would he do that?"

"I keep my sketchbooks in some carryon luggage in the back of the closet. A few days ago, I was looking at old drawings and had them scattered on the floor. I didn't have time to clean up before going out, so I shut my bedroom door. When I went to my room later, the door was ajar. I blamed it on the old building."

"Has that ever happened before?" Kade asked. "The door?"

"Not that I can recall."

"You're positive Jordan snuck into your bedroom."

"Yes, I am." Mia felt new tears prick the back of her eyes. "Am I awful to accuse him?"

"Let's back up here," Kade said. "Does Jordan know about your suitcases full of drawings? If he does, it didn't matter if he saw them."

"He doesn't." Mia let out a breath. "No one, besides me, has ever seen what's in them."

"Okay. Let's say he discovered them earlier and went looking for them last night. Why?" Kade wrinkled his brow.

"For ideas? I don't know." Mia threw her hands in the air.

* * * *

Whatever his mission might be, Kade had enough suspects to start a detective agency. *First, Rafe. Now, Poppy? Mason? Should I send more names to Beau? Starting with Jordan Reese?*

Kade recalled a recent exchange he'd had with Jordan. The man balked when Kade threw a monumental task at him last minute. Design three gowns in a week. A great challenge for the new designer. Kade would silently watch how he handled it. He never expected Jordan to react as if Kade had asked him to jump off the Brooklyn Bridge. Yet, the next day Jordan had a completely different attitude, blaming fatigue on the day before. He told Kade he'd get sketches to him in twenty-four hours.

The little bastard. He didn't do the designs! "Mia," Kade said, placing an arm around her, tugging her closer. "Did you design three gowns for the Orange Ball? It was a charity event, and I promised my friend I'd help him out. I tasked Jordan with the project."

"Yes," Mia whispered.

He lied to me! Anger welled up inside Kade. He squashed it down before he asked, "Jordan had nothing to do with any of the designs?"

"No, working on the collection overwhelmed him. He needed to focus on that project. I'd finished my part, so he asked if I minded. I didn't. It was fun. I looked up the event online and saw the women who wore my dresses. It was one of my proudest moments."

"I bet it was. They were perfect. My friends love them."

"Friends?" Mia looked up at him. Her brow wrinkled as she said, "You know the women who wore the dresses?"

"Yes, that's why I volunteered Jordan's services. Vanessa Alverez is my buddy Nash's girl. Well." He chuckled. "On again, off again girl. They're definitely on this month because they got engaged. The other two dresses were for her sister Rosa and Missy, who works for Nash. Nash called and asked if I could recommend someone to make orange, his signature color, dresses for the charity event."

"He called *you* for help with their dresses?"

"Yes. Nash knew I had connections, so he turned to me. He had no clue I'd met Jordan and could have him design the gowns."

"You gave Jordan his first test," Mia said, her voice trailing off.

"Obviously, he failed." Kade covered his mouth and sat in thought. *This is not going the way I expected. I'm confused. Is Jordan really a fashion designer or does he hide behind Mia's talents? Does Smith want me to expose him? If so, it's a pathetic excuse for a mission.*

"Enough shop talk," Mia said. "I'm sure this is a giant misunderstanding. We'll sort it out." She rose from her seat. "Now where is my sushi?"

Kade followed her to the refrigerator and placed his hands on her shoulders. She leaned back, and he felt the heat of her body melding with his. "We'll make this right, Mia." He kissed the top of her head which fit perfectly under his chin.

Mia turned and looked up at him. "I've only known you for a few days, but it feels longer. I believe you. I trust you."

Kade dropped his head, gently touching his forehead to hers. "I care about you." He wanted to hold her in his arms all night and show her how much he did. Instead, he lightly brushed her lips with his.

"That's the best you can do?" Mia teased, placing her arms around his neck, bringing him to her. Her kiss said what he was thinking. *I want you, too, but it will have to wait.*

* * * *

Mia brought Jordan to the loft as planned. Kade found it hard to believe Thursday had arrived, and he was no closer to solving his mission or even discovering what it was. He had no desire to speak with Mr. Smith. And, if he called any of the Society members, they couldn't help him either.

When Mia and Jordan first arrived, Jordan raved over the functionality and décor of the loft. Kade changed the direction of the conversation and got straight to the point. He didn't have time for bullshit and questioned Jordan's loyalty to Mia and the project. His inquiry set Jordan off into a long explanation of Tuesday night.

"Again, sorry, sorry, sorry," Jordan said, running one hand then the other through his bleach blonde spiky hair. "I shouldn't have told Mia what Poppy and Mason said. Not that I would go out on my own." He looked at Mia, sticking out his lower lip. "You and I have been a team for almost ten years. Why stop now?"

Kade stared at Mia, trying to get a read on her. She'd sat in silence as Jordan told the tale of his night, weaving his story one way then the other for the best effect. This may have been the first time Jordan really hurt her. "I agree, Mia. Why stop now? Or do you have a good reason for ending the partnership?" Kade asked.

"No." Mia shook her head, her ebony hair shining in the light as it moved with her. "I need time, Jordan. You want me to forgive you and act like everything is normal, but I need time. Just give me space. Can you do that?"

"Yes, Mee, of course. I'll give you all the space you need." Jordan walked to the front of the loft and looked out the tall arched windows. "This is a great place to work."

"Let's move you in. I'll send a truck first thing in the morning," Kade said. "Whatever you need for the project comes here."

"Really?" Jordan spun to face him. "I'm in? You believe me?"

"We'll see. Depends on what happens from here on out," Kade answered.

"I'll prove you wrong, Captain." The corners of Jordan's mouth jerked as if he was fighting a smile.

"We don't need a truck, Kade." Mia joined the conversation. "A car will do."

"You sure?"

"You have everything we need here. Are those design tables meant for us? Then we only need to bring supplies. We'll fill a few boxes. They'll fit in the trunk of a car."

"The tables are for you," Kade replied. "Damien will text you when he gets to your building tomorrow. Ten a.m. good?"

"Yes, we can be ready if we go now. I don't want to leave," Mia said with a sigh. "But we really need to get back and organize."

* * * *

Mia unlocked the apartment door, walked straight to her drawing table and threw her bag on the floor. "I guess we better get to work."

"Mia, stop." Jordan placed his hand on her forearm. "You didn't talk to me the entire way home."

"I was making plans in my head." Mia defended herself as she sorted things on her desk. "Do we have any boxes?"

Jordan took her by the shoulders and turned Mia to face him. "I will get a box. I will buy you a pet fox. I will make you a bagel with lox. Please talk to me," he begged.

Mia's mouth twitched. She bit her top lip to keep from laughing. His rhyme brought back memories of design school. On boring weekends, a group of people sat around trying to keep a child's rhyme going with their own words. Loser drank a shot of illegally confiscated liquor, usually tequila, when they couldn't think fast enough.

"I see you're trying not to laugh. You want to add the next line, don't you?" Jordan pointed a finger at Mia, and she swiped it away.

"Fine, let's sit for a moment." Mia gestured to their sofa.

"Hear me out," Jordan said as he sat. "I want to make this up to you. I'm willing to move our stuff to the loft while you go to San Francisco for the weekend."

"No!"

"Mia." Jordan folded his arms. "You should go. You'll probably have to pay an outrageous amount for a flight this late, but you'll be glad you went."

"Let me think about it," Mia replied. "Before we start packing, I want to take a shower."

"Okay, and I'll go to the coffee shop and get us loads of coffee to keep us going plus two veggie wraps."

"No visiting?" Mia closed one eye and stared at him.

"I'll be back in a half hour. Go. Take your shower."

The two parted ways. Mia went to her bedroom, grabbed some comfortable clothes and headed for the shower. *So much to consider. San Francisco, moving to the loft, Kade.* She let out a soft sigh. "Kade," she whispered.

Her thoughts switched to San Francisco. Mia quickly made a list of pros and cons in her head. *Cons. Too last minute. I won't see Kade for three days. My family will not be pleased if I do not come. Pros. Getting away may clear my head. I can still draw and sketch on the plane. I get to stay at my Uncle's hotel.*

Kaito Masuda had built the luxury hotel, The Pearl, thirty years ago. It was one of a kind and attracted business and leisure travelers from all over the world. After his death, his two sons, Mia's second cousins, took over the business. They kept the hotel's traditions alive and added a few modern updates, wi-fi and a sake bar on the roof.

Mia remembered running through the hotel's front doors as a little girl straight into a Japanese garden full of fountains, greenery and statues. Once she stepped through the Torii gate, a wooden-style arbor found at the entrance of a Shinto shrine, the real world melted away. She could play princess, battle dragons and have a tea party all in one visit. The focal point was the koi pond, centered in the middle of the garden. Paths led to a tearoom and a small shop which sold good luck charms. The main one ended at the shrine. People built Japanese shrines to hold sacred objects, and The Pearl's was decorative until her uncle died. Now it held Kaito Masuda's ashes.

I should go. No, I can't! Mia shivered, suddenly wanting to get out of the shower and into her comfy attire. She grabbed her towel after shutting off the water and stood dripping in the tub. She felt pulled in too many directions and didn't need someone determining what was best for her. *I will decide. No one else.* She wrapped the towel around her body and stepped from the tub.

As she dried her hair, Mia heard a scream. She clicked the off switch and listened. Sometimes, loud music drifted down from the apartment above, but this sounded too close.

"Oh my god, oh my god!" Jordan's voice grew louder as he reached the bathroom. "Are you done? You've got to come out here!"

Mia flung the door back, thinking it was a prank. The look on Jordan's face said otherwise. He held two folded sheets of paper in his hand. One said Mia. The other Jordan.

"What's that?" Mia pointed to the papers.

"See for yourself." Jordan gave her the one marked "Mia".

Mia unfolded hers and gasped. "Is this a joke? If it is, I don't find it funny." She glared at Jordan.

"I didn't do this. I got one, too." Jordan waved his paper in the air. "Look, it says the same thing on mine." He opened it to expose the inside.

Get out of town or.... A picture of a handgun was underneath the words.

Still unsure, Mia said, "You had time to make these while I was in the shower."

"Why would I want us out of town, Mee? We have lots to do."

Mia stared at the words. "Get out of town or someone is going to shoot us? Jordan, I am going to ask you one more time…"

"When I got home from the coffee shop, they were on the floor. Someone slid them under the door after I left. I swear." Jordan placed his hand on his heart.

"Should we call the police?"

"No." Jordan shook his head. "I'm assuming it's a prank. A one-off. But until we're sure, let's take it seriously."

Staring at the picture of the gun helped Mia make up her mind. "I've decided to go to San Francisco, Jordan."

"You have? That's great! At least you'll be away from this craziness until I figure it out."

"If I go, I want you to promise me two things."

"Anything."

"When you get to the loft tomorrow, tell Kade where I went and why."

"Don't you want to text or call him?" Jordan asked in a sympathetic voice.

Mia dropped her head and whispered, "If I do, I won't leave."

"All right. Done. What else?"

"You take these…" Mia shoved her paper into his hand. "And show him. I have a feeling Kade can help us."

CHAPTER SEVEN

Instead of heading to JFK International or LaGuardia, Mia told the driver to take her to Teterboro Airport in New Jersey, a half hour drive from the city. It was the major airport for business and luxury jets flying in and out of New York City. She'd landed there many times and was familiar with the layout.

Mia had called the Takeda concierge last night, telling whoever answered she wanted to fly to San Francisco in the morning. Within fifteen minutes, they'd texted her time and place. She'd gain three hours, so the six-hour flight would get her into California at two p.m., enough time for the Friday evening ceremony.

"Ms. Takeda," an employee opened the car door and held out his hand. "If you'd follow me."

They walked to the golf cart he'd driven to meet her. He placed her bag on the backseat, then chauffeured her to the waiting jet. "Thank you," Mia said as she slid from the seat.

One of Takeda's pilot stood in the cockpit door, ready to greet her. He gave a slight bow. "Happy to have you on board, Ms. Takeda."

Mia nodded her head. "It is kind of you to fly me home on such short notice."

"That's what we're here for," the pilot said with a smile. "Your return trip is for late Sunday night?"

"Yes," Mia answered. She planned to sleep on the way back to New York, arriving early Monday morning.

"We will take off in fifteen minutes." The pilot gave another slight bow.

A flight attendant ushered Mia to her seat where a teapot and cup sat on a table in front of her chair. "Would you like something to eat?" he asked.

"Maybe, in a bit. Thank you." Mia glanced around the plane, taking everything in. She only traveled a few times a year and with her busy everyday life, she sometimes forgot the privileges bestowed upon her. If Jordan ever flew with her, he'd never stop talking about the private jet. Perhaps it was the reason she never told him about her family's wealth. She enjoyed being just Mia, not some rich girl.

Once Mia disembarked in San Francisco, she was caught in a whirlwind of activity. A limo whisked her off to The Pearl located in the downtown area. Someone had alerted the family, and they stood in a welcome line when she entered the hotel.

"Grandmother," Mia said, giving her a bow. The tiny woman was barely over five feet, yet she packed power in her tiny frame. Since her husband and brother died, Nina Takeda was the head of the family.

Her grandmother took Mia in her arms, hugged her and whispered, "It is good to have you home, child. We must talk later."

"Of course," Mia said and kissed her on the cheek. She wondered what ominous message her grandmother had to tell.

"Mother!" Mia rushed into Ema's open arms.

"My darling girl!" Her mother clung to her…. a little too long.

Mia's dad finally intervened. "Ema, you have to share." It made everyone laugh.

"Dad," Mia said. "It is good to see you."

"And you, daughter," her father bobbed his head. "Your Aunt and Uncle O'Donnell are also waiting to see you."

Mia smiled at the couple. Her Aunt Hanna, her dad's younger sister, had married an Irishman. Their children had to answer many questions as they grew up, especially about their last name, but they didn't mind. The O'Donnells were a happy family. The first to marry outside of the Japanese culture, Hanna had caused quite a stir at the time. Now Uncle Patrick seemed like he had always belonged. Mia had grown up with her two cousins, Sean and Erin. They always looked forward to coming to The Pearl and visiting Great-uncle Kaito and his family. But lately, the Takedas and Masudas only came together for memorials. The happy times seemed to have faded away.

"Where is Erin?" Mia asked her aunt.

"She is on her way." Hanna squeezed Mia's hand. "She'll be pleased you came."

Mia and her cousin kept in touch by text, and Erin had sent a sad face emoji when Mia said she couldn't make it to the ceremony this year. Since Aunt Hanna acted surprised to see her, Erin must have told her mom.

One of Great-uncle Kaito's sons rushed up to the group. "I am sorry I am late. Ken is in a meeting. Mia, he sends his best." Koji said, bowing to her. Then he took her hand and placed a keycard in it. "It is always good to see you, cousin. Do you remember where your room is?"

"How could I forget?" Mia smiled.

During construction of The Pearl, Uncle Kaito had reserved two of the hotel's upper floors for family and insisted each family group have their own space. He didn't want them staying in hotel rooms. Uncle Kaito and his sons had lush apartments while the others had their own beautiful apartments with bedrooms, en suite bathrooms, kitchens and sitting areas. Mia's living space connected to her parents' suite.

"Good! Well, then. Let us meet for dinner in my apartment, then we'll head down to start the ceremony." Koji held up his pointer finger. "I almost forgot. Mia, your friend, Grace Edison, is here. We've put in a call to her room to let her know you're here. She should be down shortly."

"Grace came?" Mia covered her mouth. "That was so sweet of her."

"She is a wonderful girl. We appreciate her loyalty to Sean," Aunt Hanna replied. "We only wish she would get on with her life. Eight years is a long time."

"She will," Mia answered. "When the right man comes along. It's hard to find someone as good as Sean was to her."

Mia caught a flash of blonde hair from the corner of her eye. She turned to see Grace coming toward her, and tears filled her eyes. Grace might have been part of the family if a drunk driver hadn't struck and killed Sean. He proposed to Grace on that very night, the day they'd graduated from college.

"Mia!" Grace called. "I didn't think you were coming."

"Changed my mind." Mia shrugged.

Mia's grandmother approached and put her arms around the women. "You two have much to catch up on. Why don't you go to the tearoom? On me?"

"That sounds lovely, Mrs. Takeda," Grace said.

"Now Grace, I keep telling you to call me Nina."

"I'll try." Grace laughed. "But won't make any promises." She linked arms with Mia, and they started down the path to the tearoom. "Such a beautiful escape," she said as they passed the koi pond. "It never feels real in here, does it?" Grace looked at Mia with her chestnut brown eyes filled with kindness and love.

"No," Mia answered. "I've felt that way since I was a little girl." She squeezed Grace's arm. "I am glad you came."

"I try to come when I can, but I'd never miss Sean's memorial."

The hostess recognized Mia and ushered the women to an exclusive table. "Tea and sandwiches?"

"Yes," Mia said with a smile. "Thank you."

"Ooh, I love Japanese tea sandwiches," Grace said, rubbing her hands together.

Mia looked at her, studying her closely this time. She noticed that the haunted look in Grace's eyes had disappeared. *Perhaps she's finally let Sean go? Accepted his death?* "What's new in your life?" Mia asked.

"Oh, the usual. Someone tried to take over the company and my boyfriend stopped it." Grace lifted a shoulder. "Or should I say 'almost' boyfriend. It ended before it started."

Things have changed for her! Mia leaned forward. "Do tell."

"There's nothing to tell. He said he can't see me for six weeks," Grace huffed. "Like I haven't heard that before."

"He may have a good reason. What is his name, Grace? So I can stop calling him 'he'?"

"Chase Garrett, also known as Chase Young."

"He has an alias? Is he a man on the run?" Mia teased.

"Better than that. I did a little research after he left. He's a billionaire. He supposedly went undercover to help our airline."

"I can tell you're not over the lie. Can you forgive him? It sounds like he helped your dad and his company."

"I don't know." Grace folded her arms and leaned back as a server set the tea on the table. "The six weeks is almost over. One week to go. I'll decide then."

"Sounds mysterious and a little romantic."

"There's more. I'm to open a letter when the six weeks are up."

"Ooh, now it's getting good. You must call me and tell me what it says."

"Mia," Grace said as she reached out and touched her hand. "All kidding aside, what should I do? I'm tempted to never read the letter, rip it up and get back to my life."

"What life?" Mia smirked and held up her hands. "You can say the same to me, but my life, both professional and personal, is suddenly on the upturn. Let's dive in together. Throw caution to the wind."

"Oh, Mia! I am so happy for you! What's his name?"

"Kade. But we're talking about you, Grace. Don't throw the letter away. Take a chance. Open it and see what it says."

"All right." Grace lightly pounded the table. "I will. As long as you do the same."

"We're in this together?" Mia lifted a brow. "No backing out?"

"No backing out." Grace laughed.

The sandwiches arrived, and the women shared gossip, telling of their adventures with Chase and Kade. Mia confided how she doubted Jordan's loyalty after all these years but left the threatening letters out of their conversation.

"Now that you have questions about Jordan, can I be honest?" Grace asked.

Mia nodded.

"I never trusted the man. Watch your back, Mia. He may pull a fast one on you. Take all the glory for himself."

* * * *

After dinner, the family joined the rest of the guests who'd come to honor Kaito Masuda. The hotel's private hall, designed for weddings, parties and meetings, was the perfect setting for the memorial. Tastefully decorated, its round tables were covered with mint color tablecloths. Tall ladder-back chairs with padded chrysanthemum-patterned cushions surrounded them. The staff had placed an arrangement of pink and white roses in small rose gold boxes in the middle of each table. A moving glass wall system led to an outdoor garden and pond. Fire pits and torches ran along the perimeter of the water.

Uncle Patrick made an announcement. The ceremony would begin in minutes. Mia's grandmother walked to the open wall, stopped and waited for her nephews. When they arrived, Ken and Koji proceeded behind her as she headed to the pond. Each man held a lit torch. Once they reached its edge, Nina stepped to the side as one brother went to the left and the other to the right, lighting fires along the pathways on either side of the water.

Lighting your way home, Uncle. Mia watched in silence with the others until her cousins returned. Once the ceremony ended, people mingled in the gardens or returned to the hall. Mia and Grace chose to stay outside, enjoying the evening air and to watch the sun set.

"I'm leaving tomorrow morning," Grace said as they walked back to the hotel. "I wish I could stay longer but until we straighten out the mess of the foiled takeover there is extra work to do at the airline."

"I understand. It was good seeing you." Mia hugged her.

As they reached the elevator, a voice called to Mia.

"Do you want me to hold the elevator?" Grace asked.

"No, go on without me." Mia turned toward the sound of the voice. *Rafe?* Her heartbeat quickened, and it felt like her blood sped through her veins at lightning speed. *Did he follow me?*

"I thought that was you." Rafe took her by the arm. "What are you doing here?" People had grouped around them, waiting for elevators. He tilted his head towards a lounge area. "Should we get out of the way?"

"I guess." Mia felt safe in her family's hotel. *What could happen to me?* She sat in a chair so Rafe had to find elsewhere to sit. He took the seat next to her. "I should ask you the same question," Mia said. "What are *you* doing here?"

"My job." Rafe stared at her. "Don't you remember what I do for a living?"

"You never told me."

"Oh." Rafe rubbed his beard. "I'm a sales rep. I sell things to hotels. Anything from those little bottles you find in the bathrooms to mattresses for the beds."

"The Pearl is a customer?"

"Hopefully. That's why I'm here. Drumming up new business."

"At this time of night?"

"What can I say? I like the place. There's a cool bar on the roof, too." Rafe sat forward, placing his forearms on his knees. "It appears the Takeda family likes this hotel. In fact, Ben Takeda, your dad, has an office here. Any relation to the Masudas?"

An alarm bell went off in Mia's head. *Did he always know?* "My great uncle owns the hotel." *Stop! He doesn't deserve any more explanation.*

"Does he share the wealth?" Rafe wiggled his eyebrows, and Mia had the sudden urge to slap him.

"No."

"Come on, Mia. You can tell me. The Masudas own a lot of real estate. If I did a little digging, I'm sure I'd find the Takedas also do."

"Why do you care, Rafe? It's none of your business."

"Let's say I'm curious. You live in some crappy apartment building in New York City when you could live on the Upper West side or anywhere you choose in the city. Your family could buy your way into the fashion world."

"That's insulting."

"Oh, you're one of those 'I can make it on my own' type of people, I see." Rafe shook his head.

"What's wrong with that?"

"Nothing. But you've been beating your head against a wall for years. Why don't you give up and ask daddy for money?"

"I pay my own way. I'd never ask my father for his hard-earned money."

"I did a little research while I was here, Mia. Don't play dumb. *All* the Takedas have money. Your Grandmother Takeda is Kaito Masuda's sister and they grew up in a *very* rich household. Your great-grandfather amassed enough wealth to take care of generations of Masudas. Did you know Kaito and Nina planned this hotel for decades before they built it?"

No, I did not. And why did he say 'they'. It's my uncle's hotel. "Again, Rafe, it is none of your business. I haven't seen you in months and now you show up in two places where I am in one week. You admit you researched my family history. I'd call it stalking."

"I'd call it accidental." Rafe winked. "Have a drink with me. Let's go to the rooftop bar and maybe your room afterwards?"

Mia's stomach rolled over. She longed to get away from him, but his ice-blue eyes held her in place. They said he wanted something and wouldn't stop until he got it. Like always. *No! Not this time!* She struggled to stand, but Rafe was too quick.

Rafe stood to block her way and grasped her wrist. "One drink? For old time sake?"

Mia fought to be free from his grip. She twisted her arm one way then the other with no success. "You're hurting me," she hissed.

"Unhand my granddaughter!" a quiet yet firm voice said from behind her. "And get out of this hotel. Now!"

CHAPTER EIGHT

Two security guards appeared out of nowhere, and Mia wondered how her grandmother had summoned them so quickly. Rafe held up his hands in surrender. "You have this all wrong, ma'am. I know your granddaughter."

Mia rolled her eyes. *Leave it to Rafe to talk his way out of this.*

Nina gazed at Mia. "Well?"

"He's right, Grandmother. But I agree. He should go."

"You heard her," Nina said, shoving her thumb over her shoulder. "Out."

"I'll see you back in NYC?" Rafe asked so nonchalantly, it took Mia by surprise. They were kicking him out of the hotel, and he had the nerve to act as if nothing happened.

"No. Don't come by the apartment either or I'll get a restraining order." Mia glared at him.

"Fine. You're upset. We'll talk later." The security people positioned themselves on either side of Rafe. They each took an arm and walked toward the exit.

"Wait! Doesn't he need to get his things?" Mia asked.

"He's not staying here, Mia," her grandmother answered. "I was looking for you. I didn't expect to find you in a compromising situation."

"It wasn't. I can handle Rafe."

Nina narrowed her eyes. "It didn't look that way to me. Now…" She took Mia's hand and patted it. "Let's sit. There is something I'd like to discuss with you."

This sounds serious. Mia looked at her grandmother, sitting straight and proud in her seat. She always wore her dark hair, streaked with gray, pulled back neatly into a chignon bun. She still wore her wedding ring and made sure her nails were impeccably done. Mia's grandfather had given Nina the string of pearls around her neck. Her black designer dress showed off her tiny figure, and she looked younger than her years. Nina Takeda always presented her best side to the public.

"What is it?" Mia asked.

"You need to know the truth about your uncle."

"The truth?"

"How he died."

Her grandmother appeared so serious, Mia's heart pounded as she said, "Aunt Miriam passed away the year before Uncle Kaito died. I remember he was devastated. You said he died of a broken heart. Well," Mia whispered. "Everyone thought it was a heart attack."

"No." Nina shook her head. "You need to hear the truth. Your uncle committed suicide."

"What? No way. Uncle Kaito would never do that." Shocked by the news, Mia's eyes welled with tears. "Did he end his life because of Aunt Miriam?"

"No, child. She was not the reason." Nina took in a breath and slowly let it out. "He felt he'd disgraced the family."

"How? He never would…"

"It is all you need to know for now." Nina stared at Mia with soulful eyes. "It's hard to believe he's been gone five long years."

Mia's heart broke for her grandmother. She'd been close to her brother, and he'd left too soon. Mia's mind filled with questions. Ones she knew her grandmother would not answer. She watched as Nina rose from her chair and silently walked away.

Uncle Kaito had been like a grandfather to Mia. She barely saw Grandfather Takeda since her grandparents' divorce fifteen years ago. He moved to Los Angeles, keeping in touch through texts and emails. Kaito stepped in and took his place, making sure Mia had someone to lean on or go to when times got tough. The thought of his passing overwhelmed her at times. Hearing this news made it seem like his death had happened all over again. *How had he disgraced the family? What had been so bad he took his own life?*

Mia sat for a long time in the lobby, trying to recall better times. Yet her grandmother's words kept finding their way into her thoughts. *Your uncle committed suicide.* She got up and walked into the gardens, following the main path to the shrine. The area was empty of people and Mia could hold it in no longer. She dropped to her knees, placed her face in her hands and sobbed.

* * * *

Kade stared out the front windows, watching for the limo to pull up to the building. He planned to take Mia out for dinner to celebrate the move and the beginning of their relationship. Excited, he couldn't wait to tell her his plans. The black Mercedes finally came into sight. Kade made for the elevator and rushed out to greet Mia and Jordan.

Damien emerged from the driver's side, shook his head, and said, "You're not going to like this."

"Like what?" Kade asked.

The back-passenger door opened, and Jordan appeared. "Hey, Captain. Lovely day." He saluted as he walked to the trunk.

"Where is…?" Kade bent down and peeked into the empty back seat. "Mia?"

Jordan hoisted a box into his arms. "I'll tell you inside."

Kade grabbed another box, while Damien loaded a two-wheeled dolly with more of their things. He rushed after Jordan. "Tell me what?" Kade demanded as the elevator doors closed.

"Mia sent a message," Jordan answered. "Don't be mad at her. She couldn't tell you herself otherwise she wouldn't go."

"You're speaking in riddles, man! Out with it." Kade waited for the elevator doors to slide back, took the box to the front of the loft and set it by one of the design tables. "Coffee, tea or water?"

"Coffee, thanks," Jordan answered. He followed Kade to the kitchen area and sat on one of the island stools.

After he poured two cups, Kade turned to Jordan. "Start from the beginning, please."

"Has Mia told you anything about her family?"

"She's an only child and lives in the San Jose area."

"Typical." Jordan dumped spoonfuls of sugar into his black coffee. "She keeps her personal life … personal. But there are a few things I know about her. Her great uncle died three years after Mia's cousin, Sean, who was a few years older than Mia. A real tragedy. Well, both deaths were. But you know what I mean. Sean was young, in the prime of his life."

"What? When did this all happen?" Kade asked.

"Sean died about eight years ago. Her uncle, five." Jordan stirred his coffee and stared into the cup. "The family has memorials for them every year. Sean's is in May. Uncle Kaito, July. Mia goes every year. This weekend is Kaito's memorial. Mia said she wasn't going because of the show, but I thought she'd regret it. It's the fifth year of his death. I've been trying to convince her all week to go. Last night she made up her mind and left last minute. She'll fly back late Sunday night."

"Let me get this straight," Kade said, trying to keep his voice calm. "Suddenly, Mia decides to leave town. There's more to the story. What happened?"

"Nothing." Jordan held up both hands. "I swear. It's good she got out of town for a few days."

Kade didn't accept Jordan's answer but kept silent. *Something more happened. I know it.* He fumed as he worked alongside Jordan all day, trying not to pepper him with questions. "Let's knock off for dinner. I'll order something in."

"Thanks," Jordan replied, putting the last of Mia's things on her drawing table. "Don't be mad at me, Captain. I wanted her to tell you herself."

"Why didn't she?" Kade yelled. "Is a text so difficult to send?"

"For Mia?" Jordan pressed his lips together. "Yes. She likes you. I've never seen her this way before. If you would have questioned her motives, she would have stayed."

"I'd never stop her from going to something as important as a family function," Kade answered. He rubbed the spot between his eyes. *Does this have something to do with the mission?* He'd completely forgotten about his assignment all day.

"You okay?" Jordan asked.

"Yeah." Kade looked down at his phone. "Dinner's here."

Kade enjoyed Jordan's company and was glad to have company for dinner. He offered to open a bottle of wine afterwards and the two sat at the table, trading college stories and how they made a mess of things in their youth.

"So you look like a model, walk like a model and pose like a model or does that come naturally?" Jordan joked. "Yet you never wanted to *be* one?"

"Only to make money, my friend." Kade held his glass up in a salute. "Do you know how many times a day I have to avoid that question?"

"A lot," Jordan said with a laugh. "Sorry."

"It's fine. I'm used to it." Kade looked down at his phone. "It's past midnight." He noticed Jordan doing the same thing. A strange look crossed the man's face.

"No, that's impossible." Jordan shook his head. He looked up at Kade. "I got a text from Mia. Rafe was at her uncle's hotel. A few minutes ago, he approached her and asked her to go for a drink. Her grandmother threw him out of the place."

"Do you find that strange like I do?" Kade questioned. "Rafe shows up in the Village this week and now a few days later he's at the same hotel as Mia? What's the name of the place she's staying at, Jordan? Location?"

"The Pearl in San Francisco."

Really? Did Jordan say her uncle owned it? Kade was familiar with the high-end hotel. "If you don't mind, I'd like to call it a night. I'll have Damien drive you home."

"Thanks," Jordan answered and before he got to the elevator, he said, "I appreciate all you're doing for us, Kade. It's great. If Mia was here, she'd say the same thing."

Kade waited until the doors shut and tapped his phone. "Sorry to call so late, Chase. I need a flight to San Francisco, and I must leave now."

* * * *

As he boarded the plane, Kade got a text from Beau. "Sending you info on Rafe Salvadore."

"Perfect timing," Kade said under his breath.

"Welcome to C.Y. airlines," the smiling captain said, extending his hand.

"Andy! Do you ever sleep?" Kade grasped the man's hand. Andy was Chase's most trusted pilot.

"Mr. Young thought I'd enjoy a day or two in San Francisco. Whenever you wish to return, let me know."

"Andy, you're one hell of a guy. I hope he pays you well." Kade joked, knowing Chase gave Andy a good salary. Kade also planned to give Andy a huge tip after they returned to New York.

Andy chuckled yet gave no answer.

"Did Chase book you a room?"

"I'll get details after we land."

"I'll let him know I'll take care of it. How would you like to stay at The Pearl?"

Andy's eyes widened. "Why thank you, sir!"

"When is takeoff?" Kade planned to call the hotel and make the arrangements.

"Fifteen minutes?"

"Great." Kade strode to a seat, organized his laptop and paperwork on the table then made the call. A flight attendant placed the orange juice he'd requested in front of him. Kade looked up with a nod of his head and said, "Would you tell Andy we're all set at The Pearl?"

"Certainly." She smiled.

"There's a room for you, too."

"Why thank you!" The flight attendant's hand fluttered to her throat. "That is so kind, Mr. Phillips. Anything else you need?"

"I'm fine. I've got plenty of work to keep me busy." Kade swept his hand along the table. *First, I want to read the dossier on Rafe.*

"I'll let you be," she said and walked toward the front cabin.

Once in the sky, the attendant gave Kade the okay to turn on electronic equipment. He opened the file Beau had sent him on his laptop. He started reading the basic information. *Age: Thirty-two. April birthday. Grew up in Toledo, Ohio. Two years at The University of Toledo. Dropped out.*

Kade continued to the write-up from Miller Tech. They always gave a detailed report along with any facts they found. He quickly scanned the first paragraph. *He doesn't have a record. I guess that's something. Wait.* It appeared some people have pressed charges for an attempted scam, but they always dropped them. "Where do you work now? Where have you been, Rafe?" Kade read on. Hired at a company which worked as a middleman between wholesale manufacturers and hotels, Rafe traveled the country as a sales rep selling their wares.

Then something noteworthy caught his eye. Rafe had requested the west coast as his territory for the second quarter of the year. Specifically, he asked for the San Francisco area. *Seems like he got his wish.* Kade rubbed his chin. *But why?*

Kade typed Kaito Takeda into the search engine. He thought the name sounded familiar yet nothing of importance appeared. After a few more attempts and using clues from his searches, he pieced it together. "What am I thinking? Takeda is Mia's family name. Her grandmother married a Takeda. Her maiden name was…" He hit one more button and stared at a screen

of a younger Nina Takeda and Kaito Masuda.
"Masuda!"

His next entry gave Kade the information he
needed. "Kaito's a real estate mogul. Or should I say
was." The wheels in his head turned. *Rafe might have done
the same search and discovered Mia came from a family with
money or knew them in some way. He came to California to find
out for sure.* "Oh, Mia, you've kept the secret well-
hidden. I should have realized this before. You're not a
distant relation, you *are* one of the Takedas from
California. Your uncle wasn't the only one who's rich."

* * * *

After a late check-in to the hotel and four hours of
sleep, Kade felt ready for the day. On the plane, he'd
read and reread the dossier, trying to figure out if Rafe
was a threat or not. He'd practically memorized the
guy's life. Rafe had grown up in a one-parent household
with a mother and three sisters in Toledo, Ohio. Mom
worked two jobs, and the kids raised themselves. Rafe
attended the University of Toledo and dropped out
after two years.

Kade had come to one conclusion. Rafe had
researched Mia's background and found a wealthy
Takeda family living in California. He left New York on
the pretense of business, although he never told Mia he
was going there to learn more. Since he requested the
west coast, he needed to finish out the quarter before
coming back to New York. When he did, he hunted
Mia down, assuming she'd fall into his arms. When she
didn't, Rafe switched tactics.

Showered and dressed for the day, Kade went
down to the dining room for breakfast. He passed the
woman who'd checked him in last night. *Must be a shift*

change. She smiled as she recognized him and waved. "Could I have a minute of your time?"

"Sure." Kade stopped, wondering what she could want.

"I made such a fool of myself at check-in last night. When I heard your name…"

Kade held up a hand. "Not a problem."

"Well, it is if I want to keep my job. We are not to react when we check in famous guests or reveal we know who they are."

"I'm not famous."

"You're a big Hollywood producer!" she gushed. "Ooh, there I go again. I've seen all the movies you produced."

"Thank you, but I'm not famous. Just doing a job." When in California, Kade's name was recognizable. Although this far north of L.A., he'd been surprised when she recognized him.

"Again, I'm sorry."

"Don't worry, I won't say a word. I took it as a compliment." Kade chuckled as they parted ways. He walked up to the podium of the restaurant and said, "One, please."

While Kade waited for the hostess to get a menu, he glanced around the room. His eyes came to rest on a girl with long, glossy dark hair talking animatedly with the woman across from her. "Mia?"

Mia turned in her seat and blinked. "Kade?"

"Yeah, it's me." Kade rushed toward her as she rose from her seat. He didn't care who watched as he took her in his arms and lightly kissed her lips.

"I am glad to see you," she whispered in his ear. "But what are you doing here?"

"I was with Jordan when he got your text."

"You flew all the way here when you heard about Rafe?"

"I wanted to make sure you were safe."

"He's a keeper, Mia," the woman at the table said.

"Oh! Grace, I am so sorry. This is Kade Phillips." Mia placed her hand on his chest and his heart skipped a beat. "And Kade, this is Grace Edison, an old friend."

Grace was a beauty. Her dark blonde hair, parted to the side, barely touched her shoulders. The ends brushed along them when she moved. Chestnut brown eyes met his, and he caught a sense of mischief in them. At first glance, she appeared prim and proper, but those eyes told another story.

"Nice to meet you," Kade said. "Or have we already met? Your name sounds familiar."

"No, we haven't met," Grace said as she stood. "Please, won't you take my seat? I was just about to go. My flight leaves in three hours and I need to get back to my room to pack."

"I'll walk you out," Mia said, and the two women left him at the table.

Within a minute, a server came by. "Let me clear this for you, sir," he said and whisked Grace's dishes away. "Coffee? Tea?"

"Coffee is fine." Kade sank into Grace's seat, still confused. *How do I know that name? Grace Edison.* It would bother him until he solved the riddle.

CHAPTER NINE

"He is so handsome, Mia." Grace squeezed her hand. "Kade came all this way when he thought you were in trouble. As I said, he's a keeper. Go, don't keep him waiting."

"By now my entire family knows about this," Mia said as she hugged Grace goodbye. "There are no secrets at The Pearl."

"They will love him." Grace waved and headed for the elevator. "I'll text you when I land," she called over her shoulder.

Mia took a calming breath. *Maybe I can keep him to myself for a while. I can't take him to my room. It's connected to Mom and Dad's suite. His room? Too forward. Plus, my cousins check the hallway security cameras.*

Kade was eating breakfast when Mia returned. He smiled up at her. "I got fast, five-star service. Great place."

"You're probably angry with me." Mia slumped into the chair across from him.

"Why?" Kade let his fork drop to his plate. "No way."

"I didn't tell you about this." Mia waved her hand through the air. "Or the rest of the Takedas and Masudas." She bit her lip. She'd gone this far so she might as well confess. "My family has money, too, Kade. If I'd asked them for help…"

Kade held up his hand. "We've only known each other a week. It takes time to get to know and trust someone. You would have eventually told me."

Mia gave him a dejected look. "I've hidden that part of my life for so long, I'm not sure I would have."

"Would it make you feel better if I told you someone in the hotel recognized me as a Hollywood movie producer?"

Mia giggled. "Stop trying to make me feel better." She examined Kade's face. "Oh! You're telling the truth. I had no idea." A sudden urge to consult her phone came over her.

"Not too many people know producers, Mia. A few famous ones? Yeah, maybe. But me? I like to keep a low profile." Kade took a sip of his coffee. "I invest my money well."

"You've got millions," Mia teased. Kade stared at her with a playful look in his tiger eyes.

"No-o-o." Mia sat back in her chair. "You're a billionaire?" she asked in a loud whisper. Surprised by those revelations, Mia needed time to think. She never discussed money with any date or even boyfriends. They assumed she was a hard-working go getter, putting herself through school while waiting tables at a restaurant. They never questioned her background.

"Let's postpone this discussion for another day," Kade said. "I want to talk about Rafe. Is he gone?"

"From the hotel, yes. San Francisco? I have no clue."

"I have a friend who can help us. His name is…"

"Beau Miller." Mia finished his sentence.

"How'd you know?"

"Damien. He didn't tell me much but said he worked for both of you. He told me Beau owns Miller Tech in lower Manhattan."

"Okay, then I don't have to explain who he is. Saves time," Kade said. "I sent Rafe's name to him. He did a background check. The guy didn't have a great start in life. It appeared he was on his own most of the time. In my opinion, he's looking for easy money. He's scammed a few people in his past."

"So he gave up scamming and looked for a rich girlfriend instead?" Mia asked.

"Maybe. In our world today, we can gather information in minutes. I'm sure he put your name into a search engine. Once he learned about the Takedas who live in this area, he got himself transferred out here to do some research."

"Transferred? He never told me anything about his job. He disappeared from the Village, and I never heard from him again. Did he think I'd wait for his return?" Mia cocked her head, recalling their conversation from the night before. "Last night, Rafe told me he's a sales rep. Was he telling the truth?"

"Yes, he was. He travels the country. Right now, he's based in New York City. His time here is over."

"He came out here to learn more about my family?"

"Yes." Kade nodded. "Let me ask you a question. Did you ever tell him about Uncle Kaito's memorial?"

Mia squinted, trying to remember. "I may have. Oh! I must have. Rafe knew I'd be here."

"He planned to sweep you off your feet at The Pearl. Did it work?" Kade arched an eyebrow.

"No," Mia replied, playing with the silverware in front of her. "I never got to tell him my news. There's someone else." She shyly looked over at Kade.

"I hope he's good to you."

"Oh, he is. He flew all the way from New York to check on me. To protect me," Mia whispered. "Make sure I was okay." She cleared her throat. "Although I can take care of myself."

"I'm sure this man feels the same way, but he needed to see for himself." Kade winked. "Let me pay my bill and we'll get out of here."

"There is no bill. You're all set," Mia paused. "I would like to do more than get out of here. I'd like to leave the hotel and the prying eyes of my family."

"Whatever you wish," Kade replied. "How about a day on the town? Sightsee, lunch and whatever else comes to mind. I haven't spent a day like that in a long time."

"It sounds wonderful!" Mia slid her chair back, stood and offered her hand to Kade. "Let's go."

* * * *

Mia walked to the concierge station and requested a car and driver for the day. "We're all set," she told Kade. "Our car will be out front."

"I like a woman who takes charge," Kade said as he took her hand and squeezed.

A tingle went down her spine when she felt his strong hand in hers. "Golden Gate Bridge?" she asked.

Kade leaned over and whispered in her ear. "Anywhere is fine as long as I'm with you,"

A sleek silver Cadillac XTS rolled up and parked behind a row of cars lined in front of the hotel. A woman emerged from the driver's side wearing the Pearl's chauffeur uniform. "Ms. Takeda?" She held up her hand as she ran around the front end to open the back-passenger door.

"Where would you like to go on this fine day?" she asked Mia when they reached the car.

"The Golden Gate," Mia answered.

At the bridge, Mia spotted Kade's dimple. Something she hadn't noticed before. When he gave her a dazzling smile, she noticed the indentation in one of his cheeks.

During their visit to Fisherman's Wharf and lunch along Pier 39, she watched his eyes turn to a deep warm honey color when he laughed. Each time Kade looked at her, a tingle went down her spine. She felt a bond with him like no other whenever they locked eyes.

They caught a cable car and Mia insisted they take selfies as they rode through the city. Kade's muscular arms wrapped around her, pulling her tight so they'd both be in the picture or he made silly faces over her shoulder. He seemed relaxed and happy, more so than he had in New York. Mia wished she could bottle these moments and bring them out whenever he needed a lift.

"Have we done every clichéd tourist destination?" Kade teased when they returned to the car from their last outing.

"There is more," Mia answered. "But we have to save them for another day. I need to get back to the hotel and get ready for Uncle Kaito's ceremony."

"I thought it was last night?" Kade knitted his brow.

"There are two parts loosely based on Obon, the Japanese Festival of the Dead."

"Yes, I've heard of it."

Surprised, Mia asked, "You have?"

"I lease an apartment in Tokyo, remember? I don't just go there for business, I travel. I learn things. Obon is the Japanese tradition of paying respect to ancestors and loved ones who have died."

"Then I don't need to explain it?"

"Just tell me the parts you use," Kade replied.

"Last night we lit small, welcoming fires to call Uncle Kaito home. Tonight, my cousins will make one enormous bonfire, meant to see your loved one off to the netherworld. We will write messages for him and throw them into the flames. Finally we sail paper lanterns on the water to help Uncle find his way back."

"It's such a beautiful sight," Kade said, brushing his finger along her cheek.

Mia shivered as she thought. *Does he mean me or the lanterns?* Then answered, "It is."

* * * *

Back in his room, Kade headed for his closet to choose an appropriate outfit for later. Mia had asked him to accompany her to the ceremony where he'd meet the family. He wanted to make a good first impression. *Good thing I brought a conservative suit. Never travel without one.* Kade smiled as he reached for his charcoal suit, white shirt, and black, gray and white striped tie.

While in the shower, Kade got into Mission Impossible mode. He smirked at the word 'impossible'. His assignment had turned out to be the most frustrating, challenging one yet. Sure, the other guys had their fair share of danger and even a scrape with death, but Smith had given them clear missions. They had an idea of what they might face. Well, maybe not Gabe, but he figured his assignment out the first week. *I'm going on week two and still have no clue.*

After toweling off, Kade grabbed a pair of workout shorts and a t-shirt hanging on the back of the bathroom door. He slipped them on, flopped on the bed and scrolled through his phone. He hadn't come to any conclusions during the shower except to believe

Smith played them, and he could lose everyone's money.

After staring at the ceiling for a few minutes, Kade bolted upright. "Why did I come out here? Rafe Salvadore. *He's* the mission. That's got to be it. Scammer, looking for a 'get rich quick' scheme. Smith likes twists and turns. He lets everyone discover the problem. Makes it more personal. But how did he know Rafe would show up in Mia's life again?" He searched for the burner phone. "Where'd I put it?"

A pair of jeans lay across his backpack, which he'd hurriedly stuffed full of items before leaving the loft. Kade dug through the bag until he felt the slim, plastic case. "There you are. Mr. Smith, you're getting a call."

"Mr. Phillips. Enjoying The Pearl?" Smith sounded almost happy to hear from him.

"How'd you know … never mind. I called to discuss Rafe Salvadore."

"You have discovered part of your mission."

I have? "Part?"

"I'll explain after we discuss Mr. Salvadore."

"Beau Miller did a thorough investigation on Salvadore," Kade informed him.

"I am sure he did."

"Rafe's never been in serious trouble or charged with a crime. Still, it doesn't mean he's not a criminal. He wants to get rich quick. He's tried scams in the past and now has set his sights on Mia Takeda. Have you done your research on the woman?"

"I have."

"You never mentioned her when you assigned the mission," Kade reminded him. "You only talked about Jordan Reese."

"I wanted to see what you'd discover, Mr. Phillips. There is a connection."

"So, Mia's the other part of the mission?"

"Yes," Smith replied.

"Look, Smith, I don't have much time. Can you be a little more specific? This mission isn't about a fashion show or Jordan Reese becoming a designer. It's about Mia Takeda. How do you know her?"

"She's done design work for associates. Logos, banners, signage, whatever they request. My people researched her background, and I felt she was someone to watch. Her creativity and forward thinking are useful in business. She's turned down many offers to work for major companies. Her goal is to become a fashion designer. I took an interest in her and continued to observe her development. Her partner, Jordan Reese, might be holding her back or … taking advantage of her."

"I've wondered the same thing," Kade answered. "Beau is preparing a report on him. I should have it soon." His mind started piecing the facts together. *My mission is Rafe and Mia, which makes no sense. How does Smith know them both? I need more answers.* "One more question before I go. You said you took an interest in Mia. Did you have someone watching her? Is that how you knew Rafe was interested in her?" He paused, waiting for his response. "Damn, Smith, answer me!" In frustration, Kade threw himself back onto the mattress, listening for a voice. "Smith?" He looked at the screen. "You hung up on me, you bastard!"

Kade sat up and hurled the burner across the room. He stared at the wall where the phone had left a mark. *I'll pay for it.* He shook his head. "Wait a minute!"

The hotel provided a pad of notepaper and pen on the nightstand. Kade grabbed them and wrote Rafe's name at the top of the first sheet. Underneath, he wrote scammer. "There's more to this. Gabe's mission also involved a con. We both knew the woman who tried to scam him. We went to high school with her." He tapped the pen against his chin. "Blair! Damn, girl! There's no way you're involved in this. You're in jail." He scribbled her name next to Rafe's and added an "s" to scammer.

"Gabe, buddy, your ex tried to pull one over on you. If my memory is correct, you said Blair was on Smith's radar for years because of the scams she pulled with her husband and dad. Smith gave you a non-mission, as you called it, sent you home and hoped she'd try to scam you." Kade huffed. "Which she did. Maybe Smith has some secret agency assigned to watch for hackers, scammers and con artists, then protects the people they target. If I'm right, it makes more sense." He chuckled. "Maybe he thought the Society was conning him. Then he did his homework and discovered we were the real deal."

Kade spent the next hour analyzing data. *Did Rafe know Blair or her dad? Didn't grifters have their own network? If someone had exceptional talents, everyone in their circle knew of them or their reputation.* "I wish I could talk to Blair or her dad. Too bad they're in jail." He drew a line with an arrow from Rafe's name and wrote Mia. Then another one from Blair to Gabe. "Smith knew about you, my friend, before we contacted him. There's a connection, but what?"

"Rafe." Kade shook his head. "Smith's team must have tracked you to New York and discovered you hooked up with Mia. Which proves my theory. Smith is watching con artists or has a database to keep track of them. You're in his system, my man. Since Smith already had Mia on his radar, he decided I should intervene when Rafe showed up in her life."

Kade doodled on the paper, then jumped up in excitement. "Why didn't I see this before? Smith is protecting or helping women he knows on some level, even if he's never met them. Like Mia. No, that can't be it. There's no way Smith knows every woman the Society met during their missions, especially Lily." He felt like he was going in circles. "There goes that theory." Defeated, he sat on the edge of the bed. "Besides, Lily was already in Gabe's life."

Gabe and Kade had met Lily Jarvis in middle school. Even at the age of twelve, Kade could tell Lily had a crush on Gabe from day one. The three had remained friends until this day. For years, Lily worked for Gabe to stay close to him. It took the arrival of Blair, Gabe's ex, and her con artist family to open his eyes and see what was right in front of him. After eighteen years, Lily finally got her wish. Gabe and Lily were finally a couple.

"Oh, Smith, you are one irritating dude. I have some clues but need more. I'm getting closer to solving this riddle. You know what? Don't answer my questions. Make it harder than the other missions. I'll get our money back, and I swear I'll find out who you are."

CHAPTER TEN

Kade's breath hitched when he saw Mia. *Stunning.* She wore a sleek cap-sleeve black dress with a cutout under the neckline, which reminded him of a smile. As Kade grew closer, he noticed studded embellishments tastefully placed along the neckline, sleeves and each side of the waist. Her hair hung down her back, clasped with a wide barrette just below the neck. Makeup was minimal. A touch of pink on her lips, black liner and a hint of blush. "Mia," Kade breathed her name.

"Kade." Mia broke into a wide smile when she caught sight of him. "I'm glad you found me. My parents insisted I come early to greet the guests."

"Where are they? Your parents?" Kade scanned the room. "I'd like to meet them." He ran the back of his finger down her arm and swore she shivered. "You look beautiful."

"Thank you," Mia answered. "Grandmother insisted on buying me a dress for the occasion. Tailored to the knee, appropriate for the day. I guess she didn't trust me to wear the right thing."

"She rarely sees you, Mia. Think of it as a gift." Kade nudged her.

"It looks like you will get to meet her," Mia said. "She's with my mom." She stood on tiptoe to search the crowd. "I don't see my dad. He was with my cousins when I last saw him. I'll introduce you later."

Mia took Kade by the hand and guided him toward two women standing by the open wall leading outside. Both wore black. The older woman, shorter than the other, seemed to command the room with her presence. Kade felt as if an electric current ran between them. One wrong move, and she'd zap him like a bug.

"You need not bow," Mia said while they wound their way through the throngs of people. "A slight head nod will do. If Grandmother offers her hand, then take it. Do not offer yours."

Whoa! "Okay. What about your mom?"

"She'll probably hug you, so prepare yourself."

Mia stopped in front of the pair. "Mom? Grandmother? This is Kade Phillips. The man I told you about."

"Hello, Kade," the younger Mrs. Takeda said. Just as Mia predicted, she embraced him.

"Nice to meet you." Kade nodded as he stepped away. "And you must be Mia's grandmother." He resisted offering his hand and dipped his head in greeting.

"Indeed." Mia's grandmother returned the nod but produced no hand. She gave him a deadpan expression, making her hard to read.

She's a tough one. "I am honored you invited me to the ceremony, Mrs. Takeda," Kade said to Mia's grandmother.

"That is Mia's doing, not mine." Her grandmother closed her eyes and slowly opened them.

"Mother," Mia's mom intervened. "Kade is certainly invited. We're happy to have you, Kade."

"I heard it is the fifth anniversary of Kaito's death. My condolences." Kade said to the younger Mrs. Takeda, then grimaced, hoping he said the right thing.

"One never gets over the loss," Mia's mom answered. "But eventually the good memories begin to replace the hurt and help you move on. Uncle Kaito was a special man."

"I think we'll head to the garden." Mia tugged on Kade's hand. "We'll see you out there."

"Before you go, have you seen your father?" her mom asked. "We are about to start."

"I think he's helping Ken and Koji," Mia answered as she pulled Kade through the opening to the outdoors. "I am sorry about my grandmother. She does not trust people easily. It takes time. I know you'll win her over."

"I'll add it to my list." Kade teased. "Win over Mia's grandmother. I hope I don't have to do the same to you."

"No," Mia shook her head. "You already have me." She smiled at him as she glanced up at the evening sky. "It's close to dusk. Come on. Let's write our messages."

The couple walked to a waist-high, round table with beautiful custom notecards and pens on top, ready for people to write their personal thoughts. Kade had lost no one close and deliberated over what he'd write. *I should say I'm grateful I have both sets of grandparents, a brother and loving parents. No, I'll address my message to Uncle Kaito.* "No one sees these?" he questioned Mia.

"No, they don't."

Kade took a card and wrote, "Sleep in peace, Uncle Kaito. I'll watch out for the family." He folded the note in half and stuck it in the shirt pocket under his jacket.

"I was twenty-three when Uncle Kaito died," Mia said as they walked hand in hand along the pond. "The shock of his death devastated the whole family. I was told he died of a broken heart. My aunt had passed the year before, so it made sense. I assumed he had a heart attack."

"Assumed?" Kade lifted his brows.

Mia sucked in a breath. "I don't know if I should tell you this. It keeps spinning around in my head and I need to confide in someone. Last night my grandmother told me Uncle Kaito committed suicide. After all these years, I wish she hadn't." A tear ran down her cheek.

"There must be a reason she felt you needed to know," Kade replied, pulling Mia closer. "I'm sorry you have to deal with this. It probably feels like he died all over again."

"Yes, that's it. It feels so raw and new." Mia swiped at another tear trickling down her cheek. "He would still be here, Kade. He was like a grandfather to me."

Kade noticed a bench not too far from the pond. "Would you like to sit?" He guided her to the seat. "Take a minute. Catch your breath."

They sat in silence for a minute then Mia said, "My cousin Sean died almost three years before my uncle. His eighth anniversary is next May." She stared straight ahead. "Do you think I'm awful if I suggest we combine these memorials? It's become a bit much. Going to two ceremonies every year takes a toll."

I'm not touching this. "Who would you ask? Your grandmother?"

"I guess." Mia lifted a shoulder. "Christmas is the only happy time we see each other. The sad events outweigh the good ones." She finally looked at Kade. "I'm not saying there are never happy times in our family, but now that we're grown and don't live at home, those are the only times we all can see each other."

"I hear what you are saying." Kade squeezed Mia's hand. "I'm here for you. Anytime. Any place. I'll listen."

* * * *

Mia just confessed her most private feelings to Kade instead of keeping her Uncle Kaito in her thoughts. Kade filled her mind, leaving no room for anything else. As she sat silently next to him, Mia became acutely aware of his nearness. She zoned in on his steady breathing, the lift and fall of his chest. To her, it signified life. She wished to place her hand there and feel the beat of his heart. Had she really been living or was she going through the motions? She'd never felt more alive at a time and place which called for sobriety.

Kade's warm hand in Mia's made her want more of him. Guilt ran through her as she studied her surroundings. She should not be picturing Kade in various stages of undress or wearing a Scottish kilt. With one flick of the hand, she could…

"Mia?" Kade's voice interrupted her thoughts. "Is that supposed to happen?" He pointed toward the direction of the hotel.

Her cousins had set the bonfire, a huge one, which sent long flames dancing and flickering into the air. "Yes, it's started," Mia answered as she stood.

They joined the people who had gathered around the flame. Mia found her family and stood with Kade at the end of the semi-circle. Her grandmother stood between Ken and Koji, holding the torch which had lit the fire.

"Please, everyone, follow me," Ken announced, tossing his message into the fire.

The family filed past the bronze container, throwing their cards into the bonfire, ones they hoped

Kaito would receive then silently walked behind Ken toward the pond.

Hotel staff stood ready to hand each guest a rectangle lantern made from waterproof, non-flammable paper. Before placing it in the person's hands, they lit the votive candle resting in the cork bottom.

The sun had almost disappeared when they reached the pond's edge. It cast a golden glow over the garden. Nina Masuda Takeda, the head of the family, bent down and placed her lone lantern on the water's surface. One by one, the family did the same. Small groups of people walked to the pond and set their lanterns free after the family finished.

Mia glanced up at Kade, who looked quite serious, and lifted the corners of her mouth. "It is beautiful, isn't it?"

"Definitely."

Low murmurs went through the crowd as the last of the sun and daylight disappeared. Soon the lanterns would take on a new look, glowing brightly with their reflections bouncing off the dark water. It would also signal the end of the ceremony and the atmosphere would change into an elegant cocktail party with servers walking through the guests with trays of appetizers. Mia planned to escape with Kade before anyone realized they were missing.

"How would you like to view this from the rooftop bar?" Mia asked Kade.

"Should you leave already?"

"It's fine. I spoke to my mom and asked if we could slip away." Mia lied.

"As long as they're okay with it. I don't want anyone to think I convinced you to leave."

"They won't." Mia bit into her lip.

"Hey! I haven't met your dad yet," Kade reminded her.

"There will be other times. He's busy." Mia nodded toward a group of people crowded around him.

"Fine. Lead the way."

* * * *

Kade had ordered a beer and Mia held a glass of wine in her hand. They'd chosen a table with a cozy loveseat, close to the edge of the building. The view from the rooftop bar exceeded expectations. Having Mia next to him felt right. Kade didn't know how much longer he could keep a platonic relationship going. He wanted to feel her bare skin against him and wake up in the morning with her in his bed.

"What are you thinking about?" Mia nudged him.

"Oh!" Kade blinked. "You and me."

"As in a couple?" Mia teased.

"Yes."

"We could start tonight. I'll stay in your room."

Great! Let's go. "Wouldn't the cousins see? Or security might report your whereabouts."

"I don't care," Mia said, lifting her chin in the air.

"I do." *Did I just say that?* "I want your family to like me."

"They will eventually. Once they realize we're serious."

Serious. A strong word. Did I ever think of a relationship as serious? "You'll be the first," Kade confessed.

"Your first girlfriend?"

"Serious girlfriend."

"Ooh, those are big shoes to fill." Mia smiled.

Kade wished to kiss those pink lips but thought better of it. Cameras might be everywhere. Kade looked into Mia's lovely chocolate eyes. "Do you think less of me?"

"Why? Because you haven't found the right one?"

"That's one way of putting it." Kade chuckled. "And now I have." He ran his hand down her cheek, along her neck and rested it on her shoulder.

"I've put my life on hold for an awfully long time, Kade. I feel the same way."

"I had planned to take you out on Friday to celebrate us."

"I'm sorry!" Mia's hand flew to her mouth. "I handled this all wrong."

"No, you didn't," Kade answered. "But if we want to be a serious couple, we must learn to trust each other. So why don't we start simple? Where do you *really* live? I think you gave me some vague answer the first time I asked." He waved his hand in the air. "Somewhere around here."

"Atherton," Mia whispered. "Our family homes are there. The ones who still live in California spend more and more time at The Pearl."

"Whoa! Atherton? Okay, I can see why you keep it to yourself."

"You've heard of it?"

"Did I tell you I'm a billionaire?" Kade joked. "I've been there."

"We weren't always rich," Mia sounded defensive. "My great-grandfather, Toshiro Masuda, came to California with his wife in the late 1930s. He was a renowned scientist. A large company paid his way here to work in their bio-engineering department. I'm not sure of all the details because like any teen, I didn't pay attention to the story. I found it boring when the adults talked about the old days."

"You still have time to ask questions, Mia. Don't let it go before it's too late."

"You're right, Kade, I won't. But I know enough." Mia's expression changed and her voice sounded strained, "After the bombing of Pearl Harbor, people looked at my great-grandparents differently. You've heard of the internment camps?"

"Yes." A lump formed in Kade's throat.

"The president established internment camps for people of Japanese descent in the early 1940s. Army-directed evacuations began, and they relocated my great-grandparents and their infant son to one of them. My Great-grandmother Masuda gave birth to Grandmother while she lived there. By the time the country let families leave, great-grandfather had lost his passion for science. Instead, they moved into an apartment and he became the caretaker of the complex. With the money he saved over the years, he eventually bought the building. He said they'd always have a home and income. That is where it all began. Real estate was just one of the Masuda holdings. Great-grandfather believed in diversification." Mia let out a breath. "So, there you have it."

"It's shameful what the country did, yet your family's journey is a compelling story. I like a man or woman who knows what they want and never gives up. Your great-grandfather still had faith after what they did to him and his family." Kade shook his head. "I owe you my story now." He kissed her cheek. "But not today and not after what you told me. Once we have things underway back in New York, we'll talk. I hope Jordan is working his ass off while we're gone."

"Jordan! I almost forgot," Mia exclaimed. Her eyes widened when she faced Kade. "Did he tell you?"

"That you came here? Of course, he did."

"No! Did he say *why* I left last minute? What helped make my decision?"

"You felt guilty about missing the ceremony?" Kade lifted a shoulder.

"Oh, my gosh! I am going to wring his neck when I see him. Maybe he was punking me after all."

Confused, Kade said, "If I'm to help you, I need more information."

"Thursday night Jordan found two notes slipped under our apartment door. One had my name on the outside. The other, his. When I opened mine it said, 'Get out of town or' dot, dot, dot with a picture of a handgun underneath."

Kade's stomach dropped. "A threat?"

"At first I thought it was a joke. Jordan convinced me it wasn't. He got one, too. I told him to show you as soon as he got to the loft. You have your friend, Beau…"

"Who owns a cyber security firm and could sort this out," Kade finished her thought.

"Now, I'm doubting him again. Why didn't he tell you?" Mia balled her hands into fists. "I thought if I came to San Francisco for the weekend, it might help. Whoever left the note would see I left." She paused. "Do you think someone's trying to split up the team? Me and Jordan? Maybe it was Mason or Poppy? When it comes to the competition, they think we're threats. If one of us left the city because of their letters, we'd never finish the collection in time."

"You might be on to something. Or Jordan's an ass. If he did it to get you to come here, it's cruel, not funny." Kade stood and pulled his phone from his back pocket. "Give me a minute?"

Mia nodded as he walked to a secluded corner of the bar. "Andy? I hate to do this to you. I know I said I wanted to leave first thing tomorrow, but I want to move up the time. Say midnight?"

"Any time you wish to leave is fine, sir. I'll make the arrangements."

"Thanks. I know two hours is not enough time, but this is important."

"I understand. I'll text when the plane's ready."

Kade dreaded telling Mia that he had to leave right away. When he dropped the news, she looked as if she might cry. "I need to go to my room and pack. It's been a lovely evening. I'm sorry to cut it short."

"Then don't. Let me come to your room." Mia threw her arms around his neck and kissed him with such passion he came close to ditching his plan.

No! This is about her. For her. Kade grasped her arms and gently tugged them from his neck. "I'll see you in New York." He kissed her once more and headed for the elevator.

CHAPTER ELEVEN

Anger boiled up in Kade as soon as he stepped into the apartment. Two empty pieces of luggage lay open on the floor. Someone had scattered all of Mia's sketches across the kitchen table and hardwood flooring. Jordan snored lightly on the sofa, one arm over his eyes.

"Get up you little rat!" Kade fisted Jordan's t-shirt in his hands. He jerked awake as Kade pulled him up close to his face and yelled, "You sent those threatening letters, didn't you? You wanted Mia out of town so you could do this!" He pointed to the floor filled with sketches.

All other conspiracy theories flew out the window the moment Kade had stepped through the door and saw the papers scattered the floor. During his time in the air, he'd thought long and hard, wracking his brain, about who would send threatening notes to Jordan and Mia and why. He'd jotted down his ideas on the pad he'd taken from the hotel. Rafe was his number one suspect and the two designer friends came in second. Mason and Poppy could have worked together or alone. Now Jordan zoomed to the top of the list.

"No." Jordan shook his head with a wild look in his eyes. "I swear, I didn't send the letters."

"Get some shoes on. You're coming with me." Kade texted Damien, who waited downstairs. He'd picked Kade up at the airport and brought him straight to the Greenwich apartment.

"How did you get in here?" Jordan's expression took on a look of fear as he glanced around the room.

"You look so guilty, Jordan. Don't try to change the subject. If you must know, your super fell for a sob story about Mia and me. Five hundred helped some, too."

"I was just trying to get an idea. Stimulate my brain," Jordan yelled. "That's all."

"How long have you known about her private sketches? She never told you about them, so don't bullshit me." Kade heard a buzz and went to the door. He held the button which would let Damien inside the building, then turned back to Jordan. "Well?"

"I found them this week. I thought Mia was in her room, napping. I knocked, and no one answered. So I peeked in."

"Do you always walk into her bedroom?" Kade seethed.

"Yes, and she does the same. We're friends." Jordan paused, seeing the anger on Kade's face. "*Platonic* friends."

"You opened her bedroom door, saw she wasn't there and then what?"

"She'd left some sketchbooks on the floor. I thought they were from the collection and took a quick look. That girl has hung onto every drawing she's ever done. Some date back to her middle school years."

"Mr. Phillips," Damien called through the door. "I'm here."

"Open it," Kade commanded as he gave Jordan a shove.

Jordan smirked as he walked to the door. "Come in, Damien. Nice to see you." He bowed as he swung his arm in Kade's direction.

Damien made eye contact with Kade. "What do you want me to do?"

"We're taking him to Beau's."

"Hey, don't act like I'm not here. You can't whisk me away, never to be seen again," Jordan protested.

"Put him in the holding cell?" Damien asked.

Kade caught a twitch of a smile. "Yes."

"I can sue you. Have you arrested for kidnapping," Jordan shouted.

"He's kidding," Kade said to Jordan. "It's a waiting room where you'll ... wait."

"It's nice," Damien said as he faced Jordan. "There are snacks, drinks, a private bathroom. You'll be fine."

"Why must I go to the *waiting room*?" Jordan made air quotes.

"My friend Beau will run a background check on you and give me the report. I already asked him to start so it shouldn't take long," Kade answered. "Any more questions?"

"Yes." Jordan folded his arms. "What did you think I was doing here?" He nodded at the floor and table.

"Stealing Mia's designs. You hoped she wouldn't come back after you sent the threatening letters. You wanted to scare her enough so she'd stay away. Then you'd finish the project and call her ideas your own. How does that sound?" Kade tried to keep his anger in check. Jordan had played him and used Mia. What else was he capable of doing?

"Look, Kade," Jordan said in a calm voice. "Mia and I have been friends for ten years. Doesn't that count for something?"

"Not when it comes to fashion. I've seen worse. People will do anything to make it." Kade nodded at Damien. "Let's go."

* * * *

Mia woke the next morning to find her mother standing over her. "Mom," she murmured, imagining it was a dream.

"Get up, Mia. The family is having breakfast together," Ema said in a stern voice.

Mia rubbed her eyes and looked around, feeling disoriented. *Oh! I'm at the Pearl.* "Mom! Why do you sound so angry?"

"Because I am. Where did you go last night? Everyone was looking for you. Is that young man more important than your family?"

"We stayed until the end of the ceremony. Kade's flight left at midnight so I wanted some alone time with him. We went to the rooftop bar."

"You should have said your goodbyes. It's the polite thing to do."

"I know and I'm sorry."

"Fine. Do not let it happen again. I brought you up better than that."

So this is about you, not me. I made you look bad. "You did bring me up properly. Again, I'm sorry." Mia slid out of bed. "I'll take a shower and be right down." She checked the time. *Eight a.m. Eleven in New York. Should I call him?*

"Mia? You're daydreaming. Get going," her mom said, guiding her to the bathroom. "Your father and I are leaving after breakfast."

"You are?" Mia didn't want their last day filled with bad feelings. She threw her arms around her mother. "I miss you, Mom. I really do."

Ema patted Mia's back. "Is it serious, my daughter?"

"It could be," Mia responded.

"Then grab on with both hands and do not let go." Her mom released her and stepped back with a smile on her face.

"Mom!" Mia giggled. "I never heard you talk like that."

Ema sighed. "Maybe I should have let you see more of me as a person, Mia. We will remedy it now. At breakfast, I want you to tell me all about Kade Phillips, New York City and this design show."

"Really?"

"Yes, really." Ema kissed Mia's cheek. "I'll see you downstairs." When she reached the door, she called over her shoulder. "And make sure you apologize to your grandmother."

Mia went straight to the bathroom, took a quick shower, and prayed she would hear from Kade. *He must be home by now.* After she dressed, Mia checked her phone. Her heart skipped a beat. She had a text. "Landed safely. I never asked. When do you come home? See you soon." Followed by a heart emoji. Being pressed for time, she gave a quick answer. "Monday." Then added two hearts.

Kade was on her mind as she walked to the elevators. Just holding hands with him had made her warm with desire. Did he feel the same way? Mia shook her head. *Don't doubt him. He only turned down the offer to go to his room because he left. Ugh. Why do I always do this to myself?*

Friends and relatives already filled the private dining room, making Mia feel as if she ran late. Aunt Hanna was the first to spot her and they had a brief conversation about Grace. Mia assured her that Grace was happy and might finally move on from Sean and the shock of his tragic death. *With that guy, Chase?* She couldn't quite remember his full name.

Mia hugged her cousins and chatted with friends of the family as she progressed through the room. She ended up at the head table where the family would sit. Her grandmother already had taken her seat.

Might as well get this over with. Mia maneuvered around the table to get to her. "Grandmother." She bent down and placed a light kiss on her cheek.

"Hello, Mia." Nina pointed to the seat next to her. "Please, sit."

"I am sorry…"

Her grandmother held up a hand. "You did nothing wrong except forgetting to say goodbye. Your mother got upset. More than she should have. Is it past us now?" She looked at Mia with her golden-brown eyes, which always were unreadable.

"Yes, it is."

"Good. When do you leave for New York?"

"Tonight, at eleven."

"And your friend?"

"He's already left. In fact, he's in New York."

"Does he have plans for Rafe Salvadore?"

Mia crinkled her nose. "I don't think so. Why?"

"If Kade Phillips flew all this way to check on you, I assumed he did."

"Oh, Grandmother." Mia took Nina's hand. "I hope not. Rafe won't bother me anymore."

"How can you be so sure?" Her grandmother narrowed her eyes. When it came to family, Nina was a tigress.

"I'm not, but any man with pride would give up." Mia gave a nod of her head, hoping her grandmother would agree.

"You are young and still have much to learn, child. This man discovered you came from a wealthy family. Please be careful."

"I will. Don't worry."

"Oh, I *will* worry. Once you are a mother, you'll understand." Nina glanced up and smiled. "Here comes my son and daughter."

Their conversation ended as her parents, Hanna, Ken and Koji with their families joined the table. Ken went to a small podium set in the middle of the head table. He welcomed everyone for coming and said he hoped they had enjoyed their stay. If not, please send all complaints to his brother Koji, which made them laugh.

After breakfast, Mia sat with her mom and over a last cup of tea, told her of New York. "I wish you would visit, Mom. My apartment isn't the greatest, but I could find you a room nearby. I'd love to show you and dad my little part of New York."

"If your father cannot get away, I will come myself."

"Why don't you come for the show?"

"Yes, if you want me."

Mia's heart soared. She had mended her relationship with her mother and family during the weekend. She'd been just as guilty in keeping the rift going. Distance had made it easier to do. Plus, her mom said she'd come to the fashion show. "Of course, I want you to come. Dad, too."

Her mother rolled her eyes. "We'll see if he can. Work keeps him busy." Then she smiled. "But count on me."

"I'll speak to Kade. He just bought a building in Soho and is refurbishing it into lofts. He may have space there."

"Kade can afford to back you and owns a building in Soho? I had no idea." Ema placed her hand against her cheek.

"I didn't plan to shout it from the rooftops, Mom." Mia shook her head and lowered her voice. "My boyfriend's a billionaire."

"Oh, my. I am surprised."

"He doesn't look the part?" Mia teased, picturing Kade in his casual attire, shaggy, layered hair in a styled mess of curls and his tiger eyes. She liked him just fine that way.

"I am happy for you, Mia." Her mom took a sip of tea, placed her linen napkin on the table and stood. "I will speak with your father once we're on the way home. Are you finished? You need to come and say your goodbyes. You've hardly spoken to your father."

"Yes, I'm done." Mia set the porcelain teacup on its saucer and joined her mom.

* * * *

"I'm not staying overnight. I have to work tomorrow at the coffee shop," Jordan yelled.

"I'll call in for you. Say you're sick." Kade growled. "Why don't you make this easy on all of us and tell the truth, Jor*dan*. That's been your dream all along, hasn't it? Use Mia until you started a brand with your name on it."

"I told the truth. You won't believe me." Jordan flopped into a chair with a huff. "I thought we were friends, Kade."

"Depends." Kade folded his arms across his chest. "What time do you need to be at work?"

"Early shift. Seven a.m."

"Okay, I'll make sure you get there. Whatever we find, you're sleeping here. You're not going back to the apartment to clean up. I want Mia to see it."

"I need my work shirt."

"Damien will get it for you. Give him your keys to the apartment."

"Hell, no."

Kade stared him down.

"Fine." Jordan dug in his pocket and produced his keys. "You'll be sorry, Kade. Your friend Beau will find nothing on me."

"When he doesn't, I'll apologize profusely." Kade said in a sarcastic tone.

"And to make it up to me, you'll give me a loft," Jordan added.

"Don't push your luck." Inwardly, Kade chuckled but kept a stern look on his face. He was doubting Jordan's guilt. He also missed Jordan calling him Captain.

Kade returned to Beau's office to see if he had any new information. Beau's preliminary investigation had turned up nothing. Kade sat in the quiet and studied the file for hours. He'd seen all of Jordan's report cards, from first grade to design school. He learned where Jordan grew up, the clubs he joined, the sports he played. He felt a twinge of conscience when he saw Jordan played soccer like Kade had. Beau said he'd run one more in-depth search and have the findings in an hour or two. In between all the craziness, Kade had dashed off a short message to Mia. He barely had time to read her answer but smiled as he saw her shorter response. *She must be busy, too.*

His phone rang, interrupting his thoughts. *Mia!* Kade glanced at the screen. *Damn! I forgot about Ella.* "Hey, Ella, flying in tomorrow?"

"No, I'm not."

"What? Why not? I need your help."

"Hold on, let me finish. I'm boarding one of Chase's planes now. My girlfriend is driving in from Upstate New York tomorrow morning, and I want to be there to greet her. I've given everyone your loft address. I didn't want her to show up unannounced."

"Oh! That's fine. I'll have Damien pick you up at the airport." Kade rubbed his chin. "One problem. They won't deliver the furniture for the models' loft until tomorrow."

"Got a sleeping bag? I'll sleep on the floor."

"No, you won't. You'll stay with me. You can have my bedroom."

"I'd never take your room, Kade."

"I insist. Besides Chase and your mom would have my head if I didn't take care of you."

"My mom? What does she have to do with this?"

"Maureen sent me a text. She asked a few questions about your stay."

"What? How embarrassing. I'm not a child."

"You'll always be her baby, Ella."

"Fine. For the sake of not getting you killed by Chase Young or Maureen Rivers, I'll stay with you," she huffed.

"I'll see you in a couple of hours," Kade replied. "I need to finish up some business and then I'll head for the loft."

CHAPTER TWELVE

Mia unlocked her apartment door and struggled to keep the scream inside her. "Who did this?" She rushed into the room and bent down to pick up one of her drawings from the floor. "Jordan?" she called out to him. *Did someone break in?*

As she waited for a response, Mia wandered aimlessly through the room. Her sketchbooks, drawings and unfinished works lay everywhere. "Jordan!" *Ooh... I think he had an early shift.*

Mia sank onto the sofa and studied the mess, wondering where she should start the clean-up process. She always saved her work in order, oldest to newest. One carryon held her earlier drawings. The other was ongoing. It would take a while to organize it all. The more she studied the room, the guiltier Jordan became. "Why would he do this?"

Her mind skipped back to Thursday night. Jordan had pushed her to leave for her safety, yet he seemed as upset as she by the threatening notes. Her eyes flicked to the front door, recalling where he said he found them. What she saw made her heart skip a beat. Due to the state of the apartment, she'd missed it on the way in. *Another note?*

Slowly Mia rose from the sofa and walked to the spot where the note lay, shoved under the door like the others. This time there was only one note and it bore her name. *This isn't funny, Jordan.* Her breathing and heart rate sped up as she stooped to retrieve it. Hands trembling, she opened the folded paper and read, "You should have stayed away." A picture of the same handgun below the words made her shiver.

Not wanting to stay in the apartment one second longer, Mia grabbed her phone and requested a ride from her car service app. She only felt safe with Kade, so she hoped he was at the loft. If she knew how to contact Damien, she'd have called him next. The paper note felt cold in her hands, so she stuffed it into her handbag on the way down the stairs. She wanted to wait outside until her ride came. The apartment gave her chills.

To her surprise, the car arrived quickly, and Mia jumped into the backseat. The middle-aged woman turned in her seat. "Soho?" She raised her eyebrows. "Going to do some window shopping?"

"Yes." Mia bobbed her head, then looked down at her cell.

"I see you're busy, so I'll leave you to it."

Mia glanced up from the phone. "Thank you. I don't mean to be rude. I have a lot on my mind."

"I'm here if you'd like to talk … or not."

Mia would never confide in a stranger, but at that moment she felt lost and dejected. She wasn't sure if her best friend set her up for a fall. Rafe wanted her for her money. To top it off, she didn't have enough time to design a proper collection for the show. Then the mysterious notes started. Were they really threatening to kill her or just scare her? It could be a Jordan prank, but she had no clue to what was going on.

Mia found her lips moving, sound coming from her mouth even though she didn't want to say a thing. The last few days poured out of her and the woman only nodded or made a noise in her throat as Mia spoke. "What do you think?" she asked when she finished.

"First things first. You go for that man. He's into you! He flew out to California to see if you were all right? Sounds like a keeper."

"That's where I'm going … to his loft."

"He lives in Soho? A definite keeper." The woman laughed. "Now onto the serious stuff. If Rafe isn't a stalker, he's as close to one as they get. And Jordan?" She slowly shook her head. "He sounds desperate. Also seems like he doesn't do well under pressure. While you were away, he peeked at your sketches. The question is, how long has he known about your secret carryons? You need to find out. If it's been a long time, he's a suspect. He waited for the right moment. Got you out of town, then pounced on them after you left. If he accidentally discovered the drawings, it makes him less so."

"Wow, do you watch crime dramas on TV?" Mia asked.

"You bet. I can solve most of them before they do." The driver chuckled. "Well, it's been interesting," she said as she pulled up to the curb in front of the loft. "Regardless of who sent them, take those messages seriously, hon. Lots of psychos out there these days."

Way to end on a high note. "Thanks, I will," Mia said and quickly slid from the car.

Mia spotted Damien coming out of a parking garage on the other side of the street. She lifted her hand. "Damien!"

"Ms. Takeda, how are you?" Damien asked after he crossed to her side. "Going to see the boss?"

"Please, Damien, call me Mia."

"You know I can't."

"You can if you try." Mia teased.

"I'll lose my job," Damien bantered back.

"I highly doubt it." Mia smirked.

Damien pressed the button to Gabe's loft. "Want to surprise him? I know he'll be happy to see you."

"Sure." Mia smiled.

"Yes?" Kade's voice came over the intercom, making her heart flutter.

"It's me, Damien." He winked at Mia.

"Come on up."

It felt like ages since she'd seen Kade, and with the rise of the elevator, her stomach filled with butterflies. When Damien and Mia stepped into the foyer, she spotted him in the kitchen, coffee mug in hand. Kade looked rumpled, in a good way, as if he'd woken from a good night's sleep. He wore a white t-shirt and gray fleece shorts. Mia thought he looked delicious.

Kade's face wore a look of surprise. "Mia! I didn't expect you so soon."

"I needed to talk to you…"

"Kade? I just heard from…" A tall, willowy auburn-haired beauty emerged from Kade's bedroom. She wore a white, oversized dress shirt and nothing else. Her slender legs went on forever, making Mia with her five-foot four-inch frame suddenly self-conscious. The woman stopped midsentence and gawked at Mia. "Oh, sorry! I didn't know you had company."

"I was just leaving," Mia said, pointing her thumb over her shoulder. *"I'm* sorry to have interrupted." Tears welled in her eyes. Mia dug her nails into her palms to keep from crying. She sprinted to the elevator as she heard Kade call her name.

Mia hit the button over and over, knowing it wouldn't make the elevator come sooner, but she needed something to do. If she stood still, she'd break down in front of them.

"Mia." Kade placed his hands on her shoulders. "Please, listen. Let me explain."

Mia yanked away from his grip. "There's nothing to explain. In fact, it's *quite* self -explanatory."

Kade turned her around and tugged her close, holding her in an embrace she would have loved a few minutes before. "I'm not letting go until you hear what I have to say."

"Yes, you are." Mia struggled to get away, and Kade released her as the elevator doors opened. She rushed inside, but Kade followed.

"Now you're trapped." Kade chuckled. He bent down to look into Mia's eyes. "Oh, baby, you're crying. I better talk fast. The woman you saw coming out of my bedroom is Chase's sister, Ella Rivers. She's one of the models I hired to walk the show."

"So you had her practice and model one of your dress shirts last night?" Mia scoffed.

"No, she sleeps in the buff and needed to borrow a shirt."

Mia rolled her eyes. "This keeps getting better and better."

"I *am* digging myself a hole, aren't I?" They'd reached the ground floor, and Kade hit the button to his loft as he blocked her exit. "I'll ride this all day if I must."

Mia blinked back her tears, still facing straight ahead. She needed to decide. *Let Kade talk or run away?* "Fine. Speak."

"We're putting finishing touches on the loft below me. I thought it'd be a great place for the models to live while they're working on the show. Furniture is being delivered this morning. Ella should have flown in today, but plans changed. One of her friends is driving in from Upstate and she wanted to be here to greet her. When she heard about the loft not being ready, she said I should give her a sleeping bag. I insisted she take my bedroom. I slept on the couch."

Mia tried not to smile. "A sleeping bag? Do you even have one?"

"Not here, no," Kade answered. "Look, Mia. I couldn't stop thinking about you. I bored Ella to death talking about us. She can't wait to meet you."

"And the shirt?"

"She needed something to sleep in. I told her to pick something out of my closet. Hey." Kade nudged her. "Didn't I ask you to be my girlfriend? It's a big step for me. I hated leaving you in San Francisco." Kade gathered her in his arms. He touched his forehead to hers.

Mia lifted her head and was a breath away from his lips. She wanted him to kiss her and never stop. Kade drew her closer and gently placed his lips on hers. She heard the elevator doors open and giggled when she saw Ella, who must have dressed quickly, and Damien waiting to board.

"Mia! I am so-o-o sorry! Kade and I are old friends. Trust me. Nothing happened." The words poured from Ella.

"It's fine." Mia held up her hand. "Kade explained."

"I'd never jeopardized this assignment. It's my first runway job." Ella's eyes widened with hope.

"I believe you and thank you for doing this."

"I'm going down to the loft to wait for the delivery and my friend," Ella said with a smile. "I think you two need some alone time."

"Call if you need me, boss." Damien saluted and joined Ella on the elevator.

Kade took Mia's hand. "I've got coffee and bagels. Hope that's okay."

After plating their food, they settled in at the kitchen island. "Now," Kade said. "There is something you wanted to tell me?"

* * * *

Mia stared at him with soulful brown eyes. "It's Jordan."

After what happened, Kade wanted to wrap his arms around her and never let go, but this sounded serious. *First things first.* "What did he do now?" *He couldn't have done anything recently. He's been in our custody since yesterday afternoon. Damien dropped him off at work a couple hours ago.*

"I can't even say it."

Kade rubbed her back. "Take your time."

"I'm not one hundred percent sure, but he staged a break in at our apartment."

Wow. I didn't think she'd go there. "Was anything taken?"

"No, I don't think so." Mia placed her hand over her mouth. She took a deep breath and continued. "I think he wanted it to look like Poppy or Mason had done it. He'll blame one of them when he gets home from work. My sketches were all over the place. I never checked to see if something was missing once I found another note on the floor. He put it close to the door to make it look like someone shoved the letter under it."

"What did it say?" Kade seethed. He'd searched the room and hadn't found a letter. *I'm positive I saw nothing. There was no letter.*

Mia slid from the barstool and went to her bag. She rifled through until she came up with the crumbled piece of paper.

"Is that it?" Kade asked. "May I see it?" *And get it to Beau for fingerprints?* He'd never seen the other notes firsthand.

Mia handed him the crushed paper. He untangled it and read aloud, "You should have stayed away." Same picture of a handgun was underneath the writing. "It wasn't Jordan." Kade shook his head.

"What?" Mia's eyes widened.

"Let's say I'm pretty sure it wasn't Jordan." Kade didn't want to get her hopes up. "He's been at Miller Tech since yesterday afternoon. Damien drove him to work this morning."

"You went to the apartment?"

"As soon as I landed. I thought the little bastard was up to something."

"And?" Mia lifted her brows.

"Saturday night he had a meltdown. According to Jordan, he saw your drawings for the first time when he went to your room last week. He thought you were taking a nap, opened the door and saw them laying on the floor. He figured he had the entire weekend to study them for ideas, but there were two things he didn't plan on. Falling asleep before cleaning up and me catching him in the act."

"Are you sure he discovered my drawings just last week?" Mia asked.

"Yeah. He was pretty upset when I caught him. Jordan thought he'd lose you as a friend. I'm giving him the benefit of the doubt. Which brings us to…"

"Who did this?" Mia's relaxed expression changed to concern. "It's not a joke, is it?"

"I don't think so." Kade held up the note. "Mind if I keep this?"

"It's all yours." Mia took his hand. "Can we stop talking? Let's sit on the loveseat. Please, just hold me."

"I thought you'd never ask," Kade answered, tucking away his anger and detective skills for now. Mia needed him and that was more important.

* * * *

Mia snuggled against Kade and placed her hand on his chest to feel his steady breathing. Each breath he took calmed her. She had no idea how long they sat without saying a word, yet she was grateful for the time. Mia sat up and faced Kade. "Why is this happening? I finally get what I want, and my world falls apart."

"Did you ever hear the old saying be careful what you wish for?" Kade chuckled and stroked her cheek. "Don't go there. You deserve this and so much more. I promise you. I'll fix this."

"*We* will fix this." Mia corrected him. "Where do we begin?"

"Do you know what time Jordan's shift ends?"

"Let me check." Mia grabbed her phone from the coffee table in front of them. "Three."

"I'll ask Damien to pick him up and bring him here. Why don't you go over to your workstation and check it out?" Kade tipped his head toward the front of the loft. "Jordan did a good job of organizing your space. While you do that, I'll check on the furniture delivery."

"Ooh, I'd love to see it."

"When it comes, I'll let you know. We'll go down together. Ella would love your input."

Will she? Some women would not. "I'll go as a silent observer, unless she asks for an opinion." Mia smiled as Kade drew her closer. *Kiss me! Please kiss me.*

"Do you need anything before you start to work?"

Mia nodded. "You."

"You always have me." Kade placed his lips lightly against hers, soft and warm. She melted into the kiss, every nerve tingling, each part of her womanhood responding. He deepened the kiss and her head spun, scrambling her thoughts.

Kade leaned back. "If we keep this up, we won't get any work done."

"True." Mia playfully poked him in the chest. "But once I finish the collection, I intend to celebrate with you. Like this."

CHAPTER THIRTEEN

Jordan walked up to Mia with a sheepish grin on his face. "Mee? Forgive me?" He still wore his navy-blue Perks work shirt, which had a coffee stain on the front.

"It depends," she answered, tapping her sketch pencil on the desk.

"On?" Jordan cringed.

"When you discovered my drawings. And don't lie. I can tell when you are."

"As I told Kade," Jordan said, running his hand over the top of his bleached blonde hair. "I thought you were napping. When you didn't answer, I peeked in to see if you were there. That's when I saw your sketches on the floor. You must have left in a hurry. It's not like you to leave your things all over the place. I assumed they were part of the collection and you planned to get back to them. I took a quick look. To my surprise, I found a stash of outstanding fashion drawings going to waste. Why didn't you show me?"

"They weren't good. Not up to my standards."

"Not good enough? Mee, a lot of those are worthy." The corners of Jordan's mouth twitched. "Do you forgive me?"

"Not yet. I have one more question. What did you do this weekend?" Mia lifted a brow and stared at him.

"I panicked! Since you'd left and wouldn't catch me in the act, I pulled both carryons out to the living room and sorted through them. I wanted to get some ideas. I never felt this much pressure in my life." Jordan's eyes welled with tears.

Mia took a deep breath and let it out. "I believe you." She glanced at Kade for confirmation.

"His story checks out," Kade replied. "He has no priors or arrests. And he played soccer in high school. Can't be all bad."

Jordan swung his head toward Kade. "What does soccer have to do with this?"

"I also played."

He held his hand up for a high-five, and Kade slapped Jordan's palm. "We're cool?" Jordan asked. "I get the loft?"

"Hold on now." Kade chuckled.

"Hello? Am I missing something?" Mia crinkled her nose. "Soccer? Lofts?"

Kade strolled to her desk and leaned against the edge of it. "Do you remember I told you I met my best friend, Gabe, playing soccer?"

"Oh, yeah." Mia rubbed between her eyes. "It feels like ages ago."

"And," Jordan said. "I asked Kade for a loft if it turned out I was not guilty. Which I am, by the way. Not. Guilty. Well, except for looking at Mee's hidden treasure behind her back."

"You know what, Jordan?" Kade grinned. "You may get a loft after all."

"Really?" Jordan appeared more like himself. "Mia will come, too. We're a team. And she'll be close by. Only an elevator ride away." He wiggled his eyebrows at Kade.

"Stop." Mia finally gave in and smiled at him.

"Mee!" Jordan held out his arms.

Mia slid off her stool and went in for the hug. "We're still not one hundred. There's a giant mess in the apartment."

"I'm sorry."

"I have a system."

"Of course, you do. And I will help you organize and get it back to normal. I promise," Jordan said.

"I'll help, too," Kade added.

Jordan cleared his throat. "I'd also like to say, you can arrest me anytime, Captain, I had five-star service and the apartment Beau gave me for the night was to die for."

"Glad you survived," Kade answered. "Now, if you'll excuse me, I have work to do and so do you."

Once Kade walked into his bedroom, Jordan took Mia's hand. "Tell me everything. Did you sleep with him yet?"

"No." Mia shook her head. "I told you we're waiting until you and I finish the collection."

"Then let's get to work." Jordan slid over to his desk, which faced Mia's. He checked his station, hopped onto the stool, and looked up at Mia. "You been here all day?"

"Yes."

"What have you been doing?"

"Working, like we're supposed to." Mia gave him the evil eye or at least tried.

"Okay." Jordan held up his hands and rolled his eyes. "I'll get to work."

Mia didn't mean to hurt his feelings, so she said, "I met Ella Rivers, one of the models. She was here when I arrived."

"No!" Jordan stared at her, then glanced toward Kade's bedroom.

"It's not like that. She's the sister of Kade's friend. Ella's nice. Kade is furnishing the loft below us for the models to use while they're here. The store delivered the furniture today, and we went down to see if we could help."

"She wasn't a bitch?"

"Absolutely not. She's grateful for the opportunity. This is the first time she'll walk the runway."

Jordan brought his hand to his head, covering one eye. "Please tell me she's had *some* experience."

"Catalog work. Department store flyers and online. I can show you if you want." Mia gestured to her computer.

"Later. We really need to work."

They always worked with classical music playing softly in the background. Kade had helped Mia link her phone to his system, and she started the track. Her heart pounded as she waited for Kade to return and begin the plan they'd put in place. She'd felt guilty when they first discussed it, but they had to do it. *I did my part. Forgave Jordan. Put him at ease so we can catch him off-guard. This is the last test, Jordan, and I hope you pass.*

* * * *

Kade called Beau as soon as he got to the bedroom. "Hey, Beau, any news yet?"

"We pulled fingerprints from the paper, but they're yours and Mia's. Thank her for cooperating."

Damien had driven Kade and Mia to Miller Tech earlier in the day. A security officer took her fingerprints for comparison. Beau already had Kade's.

"It's not surprising to find no other fingerprints," Beau continued. "But we're not giving up. Blake has a few ideas."

"Thank your brother for me," Kade said. "I agree. The fingerprints were a longshot."

"I'm glad you brought the note to me. Gives us something to go on." Beau paused. "Have you spoken to Smith since this happened?"

"No, I guess I should."

"From what you've told me, this Rafe Salvadore is a person of interest. Smith thinks so, too. He's probably your mission. It sounds like Rafe was on his radar long before we got involved with him. Just like Blair Winters."

"I thought the same. Has Smith been watching them, keeping tabs on them for years and if not years, for how long? Here's another question without an answer. Are Blair and Rafe connected somehow?"

"Probably not. But with Smith, you never know. If you want my opinion, he's set up a covert agency for this sort of thing."

"If Smith has some secret operation watching grifters, why doesn't *he* do something about it himself?" Kade sucked in his anger. "How did he know we'd call, and he could give us these assignments?'

"Right time and place?" Beau answered. "Look, we know where Rafe lives and I've got a person watching his apartment, waiting for him to come home. Funny thing, he hasn't checked in yet."

"Really? I assumed he came back to New York."

"If he truly is a con artist, he may have changed addresses. We'll call the company where he works to get more information. If you need anything, I'm a call away."

"Same here," Kade said as he ended the call. He glanced toward the front of the loft. "Showtime." He put on his game face and strode out of the bedroom, heading straight for Mia. "We got something."

Mia gave him a look of surprise. "Beau found something on the letter? Fingerprints?"

Jordan looked at Mia, then Kade. "What are you two talking about?"

"You don't know?" Kade stared at him. "You're the one who told me about the threatening letters supposedly shoved under your door."

"They were! And I never gave them to you. How could you possibly analyze something you don't have?" Jordan pointed at Mia. "Were there more? Did we get more threats?"

"Not you." Mia shook her head. "Just me."

"I'll call Mason, then Poppy!" Jordan yelled. "No, I should call Poppy then Mason. Whatever! One of them is guilty."

"Jordan! Stop." Mia demanded. "Why are you so sure one of them left the note?"

Jordan groaned. "Full disclosure? I saw them this weekend at the bar. I told them you were in San Francisco. Think, Mee. It was the perfect setup. They're so jealous of us they'd do anything to scare us away. When I said you were in California, Poppy's eyes lit up. She asked if you were gone for good. Mason laughed and said it was about time you left me." Jordan scratched his chin. "I told them you'd be back Monday. You should have seen the look they gave each other. Maybe they're in this together. They left those letters for us Thursday night and got upset when it didn't work."

"You could be right," Mia answered and faced Kade. "Well?"

Kade studied Jordan's facial expressions and body movements while he spoke with Mia. He appeared surprised about another note with no signs of guilt. Unless he was an excellent actor, Kade could almost exonerate him. But until he had proof positive, Jordan would stay on his radar. "He's getting closer to that loft." He winked at Mia.

"I am?" Jordan pounded his desk and let out a loud whoop. "What do you need? I'll do anything, answer anything, help you set up Poppy and Mason. Whatever you want." His expression became serious. "What did the note say, Mee?"

"It said I shouldn't have come back with the same picture of the gun."

"No way!" Jordan's eyes met Kade's. "You saw nothing suspicious when you were at the apartment, right?"

"I did not." Kade shook his head.

"Neither did I."

"You follow your lead, Jordan. Don't let on anything is wrong when you speak with Poppy or Mason. Got it? Bait them. See what they say." He planned to steer Jordan in the wrong direction and keep him out of the crosshairs. He now had his number one suspect. And his name was Rafe Salvadore. *I need to catch him in the act. But how?*

"I'm willing to do anything, too. I want this over." Mia set her pencil on the desk. "I can't concentrate." She got down from her seat and slipped her hand into Kade's. "Let's talk."

Kade checked his watch. "First, we order dinner." His phone buzzed, and he saw the Society's pyramid in a text message from Chase. "Order whatever you want. I'll pay for it. I need to take this." He slipped a credit card into Mia's hand before going to the bedroom.

If no one sent an 'inconvenient time' message, his phone would ring any minute. Kade sat on the edge of the bed, waiting to see what happened. The conference call would include all six society members. Within a minute, his cell rang. "I'm here," he said, listening for the other voices.

"What's up, Chase?" Beau asked.

"There better not be a problem." Kade heard Nash's voice and smiled. "If there is, I'll kick some ass. And we know who I mean."

"Smith?" Finn chuckled.

"Gabe, you there?" Kade questioned.

"Yeah, just listening."

"Hey, we need to talk later."

"You can talk to him in person," Chase interrupted the banter. "Smith's called a meeting for Friday."

"Friday?" Kade growled. "I don't even get two weeks to finish my assignment?"

"Maybe he thinks you'll complete it by then," Chase answered.

"He must think you're on the right track, Kade," Gabe said.

"The sooner we get our money back, the better," Nash replied. "Is this what the meeting's about, Chase? The money?"

"Come on, Nash. You know better than to ask me that question. Smith never tells us anything."

"Son of a bitch," they all said in unison.

"I'm setting up a flight schedule so text me your preferences by Wednesday. You need to be here by three p.m. on Friday."

"Kade?" Beau said. "We'll coordinate and go together."

"Sure thing," Kade agreed.

"I hope to see you then," Chase said. "Good luck to us. We're the Six!"

"From the bottom to the top!" they shouted.

Kade disconnected from the call and went out to the sitting area. Mia sat in her favorite brown and white buffalo plaid loveseat. She patted the spot next to her when she saw him. "Dinner should be here in a half hour," she said after he sat. "I want to talk to you about something. Say nothing until I'm finished. If I know you like I do, you'll say no." Mia lowered her voice so Jordan couldn't hear. "I don't think Poppy or Mason sent the letters. You're trying to keep Jordan out of this, and I thank you for that. We both know Rafe is doing this. I want you to use me as a decoy. Let's set him up."

Her hand came toward him as Mia covered his lips with her pointer finger. "Don't say anything yet. Think about it."

Kade gently took Mia's wrist and pulled her hand away from his face. He placed a kiss inside her palm. "You are wonderful and brave. But if you think I'm letting you anywhere near that bastard, you're dead wrong."

CHAPTER FOURTEEN

Mia tossed and turned, dozing and waking through the night, her mind full of plots and plans. When the first light came through her window, she kicked off the sheet and rolled from her bed. *I need to do something! Rafe is my problem.* She headed to the shower to get ready for the day.

When Mia walked out to the living area, she found Jordan at his desk. "Hey, Mee, couldn't sleep?"

"No, too much on my mind. Looks like you couldn't either."

"Yep, my brain is on overload. But we've made progress, don't you think? That should help calm our nerves."

"It's not the collection that's making me crazy. It's Rafe."

"Oh." Jordan pointed at her. "I see the look on your face. You're up to something. Kade won't like it."

"Kade won't know," Mia said. "When do you go into work today?"

"I have an evening shift. You need to stay at the loft until I'm done. Kade doesn't want you here alone."

Tonight is perfect. "Do you think Rafe is watching me every minute of the day?"

"Might be hard to do, but maybe." Jordan shrugged. "All the more reason to have someone with you at all times. Are you done in the bathroom? I need to get ready. Damien is picking us up at eight. We meet the pattern makers and cutters today."

"It's really happening, isn't it?" Mia shivered with excitement. "We going to see our drawings turned into real creations."

"Yep," Jordan said and gave her a kiss on the cheek as he went by. "I hope Kade's serving breakfast. I'm starving."

* * * *

"Mr. Phillips."

Kade put in a call to Smith as he prepared a simple breakfast for himself and his guests. He'd put the burner phone on speaker so he could work in the kitchen. To his surprise, Mr. Smith picked up on the first ring.

"Why are you having the Society meet on Friday?" Kade asked, trying to control the anger in his voice. "You barely gave me two weeks to finish the mission."

"I am sure you will complete the assignment by then."

"Okay, let me get this straight. You never gave me instructions, but I'll finish by Friday?" Kade pushed the start button on the coffeemaker and took plates from the cupboard.

"I believe we discussed Mr. Salvadore and Ms. Takeda when we spoke."

"Yes, we did, but you never told me what to focus on. One or both? The guy is a con artist. He followed Mia to San Francisco. Tried to get her back as his girlfriend. She didn't want any part of him. It's over. She's safe."

"Is she?"

"Look, Smith, I have Beau on his case. We don't know if Salvadore came back to New York or not. Rafe hasn't shown up at his apartment. Beau's checking his work status."

"And Ms. Takeda?"

"She will work on her collection from my loft along with her partner until it's done. I can watch over her."

"Is Mr. Reese a suspect or accomplice in any of the things we discussed?"

"If you're asking about his work relationship with Mia, Jordan is a true partner. His nerves got the better of him and he did something stupid. His story checks out. According to Mia, Jordan didn't like Salvadore from the start. I doubt he'd team up with him. So, to answer your question? No, he's neither a suspect nor an accomplice. Mia and Jordan are a team. I will see my assignment through till the end, Smith. Their collection will be on the runway at the August show. That's what you originally told me when you gave me the lame assignment. Move Jordan's show to August, and so I did."

"Good to hear."

"But you never meant that to be the assignment. Am I right?"

"Correct."

"You waited to see if Rafe would show up again. You wanted Rafe caught and Mia protected."

"I am happy it worked out that way."

"But you weren't sure it would, so you left me clueless."

"As I told you before, Mr. Phillips, all things come to those who wait."

"You sound like your talking more about yourself than me," Kade replied.

"Your fellow society members may believe I am omnipotent, but I am not, Mr. Phillips. They sometimes expected me to pull rabbits out of hats for them. This was a give and take deal. Remember that."

"Fine. So in your eyes and mine, I've completed my mission. When the guys and I show up Friday, you'll give our money back?" Kade felt good about the outcome. Smith said Rafe was his target, and he'd done his best to expose him. Jordan was a subplot, easily exposed and fixed. Mia needed protection, and he was there to provide it. Case closed.

After putting the finishing touches on breakfast, Kade realized he'd waited longer than he should have for a response. "Smith? Do we get out money back?" He huffed. "Are you even there? Damn! He hung up." He made a fist and shook it. "Again!"

His cell buzzed, informing him someone was at the loft entrance. Kade checked the camera and saw Mia and Jordan standing on the sidewalk. "Come on in," he said into the phone as he released the lock.

Kade strolled to the elevator to wait for them, suppressing the urge to pluck Mia right from the cubicle and carry her to his bedroom. He couldn't stop thinking of her offer at The Pearl. *Which I turned down like an idiot.*

The doors pulled back, exposing Jordan and Mia on the other side.

"Captain." Jordan nodded and continued into the loft.

"Kade," Mia said and rushed into his open arms. "I missed you," she whispered, then stood on her tiptoes to kiss him.

"How soon before you finish the drawings?" Kade asked. "I can't wait to feel you in my arms."

"Friday, the latest. I can't wait either." Her dark brown eyes sparkled.

Friday! Damn, I won't be here.

"We'll celebrate that night. Okay?" Mia fluttered her eyelashes and laughed.

Her laughter filled him with joy, yet his stomach plunged to his feet as he asked, "Can we make it Saturday night instead?'

Mia's expression changed so quickly, it broke Kade's heart. "Do you have plans?" she asked in an accusing tone.

"I made them long ago," Kade lied. "I'm going to my friend Chase's house. He lives in North Carolina. A quick overnight."

"You'll need to tell me more about Chase and your other friends. You are loyal to each other. I can tell. But could you cancel this one time?"

Kade searched his mind for something Mia would accept as a good reason for going. Meeting with the ominous Mr. Smith wouldn't work. "I'd love to, baby. I'd rather be with you than a bunch of frat boys. But it's important I go. One reason is Nash's wedding. He's turning into a groomzilla. If I'm not there, who knows what he'll do." Kade hoped to make her laugh but watched Mia's facial expression change to one of sadness.

"Oh," she said

"Is something wrong?" he asked. "Did I overdo it with the 'groomzilla' comment?"

"Nothing is really wrong. And no, the comment was funny." Mia slipped her arm through his and walked Kade toward the kitchen where Jordan was helping himself to breakfast. "Is this the Nash I designed the gowns for?"

"Yes, and he's in for a surprise when I tell him my girlfriend designed those dresses, not Jordan." Kade glared at Jordan.

"I'm sorry," Jordan said with a mouthful of bagel.

"It's fine, Jordan," Mia answered. "It has nothing to do with the dresses." She looked up at Kade and said, "I know his fiancée, Vanessa Alvarez."

Shocked by her announcement, Kade stopped and faced her. "You do? How?"

"We were roommates at Florida State freshman year. I was only seventeen. Vanessa turned nineteen before Christmas. I was in awe of her and felt she was already a woman of the world. So full of life, popular, yet she always had time for me. I left after freshman year, never to see her again until I looked up the charity event. There she was, the Vanessa I knew and loved, wearing my dress."

"Wow. Small world. Why didn't you contact her?"

"Too embarrassed." Mia hung her head. "Vanessa tried to stay in contact, but I thought she was just being nice."

"Van's not like that." Kade furrowed his brow. "She'd love to hear from you even if it's ten years later."

"And tell her what? I was a shy, awkward teen who didn't appreciate her friendship?"

"Yeah, exactly that." Kade poked her.

"Please don't tell Nash who I am. If she's in your life, she'll be in mine. I need to make amends."

"Okay. After the show, we'll get together with them. I won't say a word except they'll meet my new girlfriend."

"Coffee, lovebirds?" Jordan turned from the coffeemaker, two mugs in hand, and smirked at them.

"Sure, thanks." Kade took the cups and gave one to Mia.

"Stop it, Jordan." Mia giggled.

"Well, you two sound like an old married couple already." Jordan rolled his eyes. "When everyone gets here you better both put on your professional pants."

* * * *

After breakfast, the loft filled with people who streamed in and out for the rest of the day. Mia and Jordan met with the pattern makers, a courier delivered the fabric, and Ella arrived with her friend Rachel, introducing her to the group.

Mia's heart swelled with pride as people gushed over the drawings. The show finally became a reality in her mind. She felt Kade's arm wrap around her shoulders. "You okay?" he whispered in her ear.

"A little overwhelmed, but in a good way," Mia answered. "This is a dream come true. Thank you, Kade."

"Don't thank me, thank Jordan. He's a good salesman."

"Yes, he is. Look at him. He's in his element." Mia watched Jordan explain to one of the team exactly how he envisioned the outfit, joking and laughing as he made his point. "I'm glad he had nothing to do with those letters." She glanced up at Kade. "You've exonerated him, right?"

"Yes," Kade said under his breath. "But I'm still keeping an eye on him."

Mia gave him an exasperated look. "If you don't think he's guilty, then why?"

"I can't take any chances when it comes to you." Kade kissed the side of her head and she felt his warm breath against her skin.

"Hey, you two," Ella said as she approached with Rachel. "Let's have dinner tonight. I want to show you my list of models for the show and see if there's anything else I can do."

"You've been great, Ella," Mia said. "Can I take a raincheck? How about lunch tomorrow?"

"Sure." Ella nodded. "If you don't need us any longer, Rachel and I will head out. I'm starving!" she laughed. "Not something a model would say, is it?"

Kade chuckled. "No, but you're not the typical model. Have a good dinner." He nodded at them, then turned to Mia with a serious face. "Now who has plans they can't break?"

"I planned to tell you, Kade. We've been so busy." Mia blew a stray hair away from her eyes. "I want to go back to the apartment with Jordan. I need some down time."

"Doesn't Jordan have to work?"

"Yes, Jordan does," Jordan answered, walking up to the couple. He placed his hands on his hips. "What are you up to, Mia?"

"Nothing. I wanted an hour to myself to gather my thoughts."

"You'd be alone in the apartment. We decided you should be with someone at all times." Jordan stared at her.

"Fine! I'll come to the coffee shop with you."

"I can meet you there," Kade said. "After you've had your alone time."

Mia's mind whirled until she found an excuse. "Could Damien pick me up? I'll come back here until Jordan's off work. Now that I have his number, I'll text him when I'm ready."

"Sounds like a plan," Jordan replied. "I need to get going. Shift starts in an hour."

"I'll let Damien know you're ready," Kade answered.

"Tell him I'm coming, too," Mia said, trying to keep cool. She didn't want Kade to suspect anything. Tonight she'd set her plan into motion. Expose Rafe and end this once and for all.

* * * *

"Don't walk so fast!" Mia jogged to catch up to Jordan.

"I'll be late for work if I don't. Can you please try to keep up?"

"My legs aren't as long as yours," Mia complained, then laughed. "How many times have we had this conversation?"

"Five hundred ninety-two," Jordan answered. He stopped and turned on his heels. "Mee, if you're up to something, tell me now. I can't watch you every second in the shop. Sit close where I can see you." He pulled her to him, enclosing her in his arms. "You are my best friend. I want nothing to happen to you."

"You're making it sound like I might die or something." Mia teased.

"Well, maybe. You never know."

Mia poked him in the chest. "Stop joking."

"Fine. I want to tell you something and you *have* to promise not to tell Kade."

"O...kay."

"No, really. Promise." Jordan glared at her.

"I promise."

"I learned a lot while I was at Miller Tech. Also, I have good hearing."

"You mean you're good at eavesdropping."

"Yes, there's that."

"So," Mia said as they started to walk again. "What did you learn?"

Jordan quickened his pace, and Mia tried to keep up with longer strides. "Beau Miller is a genius," he said.

"He is Kade's friend. They went to Harvard, so I don't doubt it."

"Yes, agree. But I mean at analytics. Problem solving. Seeing beyond what's there. You don't learn that. It's in you."

"Wow. You heard a lot."

"Yes, I did. And here's the secret part. Seems like there's an agency out there, one we don't know about, that watches for criminal activity. Especially con artists. Scammers. Grifters. And Rafe may be on their list." Jordan opened the door to the coffee shop. "Let me punch in and I'll serve you so we can keep talking."

"Like we've never done that before." Mia smiled. "I'll get a table." She chose one by the window where someone could see her. She pulled out her tablet and set it up like she would work there while waiting for Jordan.

Within five minutes, Jordan showed up at the table with her coffee and a slice of iced lemon loaf cake. "I guessed. Please tell me you didn't want the red velvet loaf."

"I love them both equally," Mia replied. "Now, since there aren't too many customers, can you sit for a moment?"

"Yeah, I told Annie we had a fashion emergency and needed to confer."

Annie, the night manager, was an aspiring actress who longed to be on Broadway. She'd gotten parts in some off-off Broadway plays and understood the struggle to make it big. Mia waved to her and smiled.

"You were telling me about this secret agency," Mia reminded Jordan. "Which I highly doubt exists."

"Really?" Jordan widened his eyes and leaned back. "Where have you been? Don't you read anything online except fashion blogs? Have you ever watched shows where someone is tracking your every move? One series even had a computer spit out a name of a perpetrator before they committed the crime. And don't get me started on governments."

"Fine. So they exist. What does that have to do with us or Beau and Kade?"

"It's where they got their intel! They spoke about some man who passes along the information to them. That's what I've been trying to tell you." Jordan leaned over the table and said in a quiet voice, "Beau and Kade think Rafe is a grifter."

"What? No. He told me he's a salesman."

"It's his day job or cover," Jordan smirked. "He's out to con someone, and they think it's you. Here's the million-dollar question. Why?"

Mia swallowed and heat slowly crawled up her neck to her cheeks. "There's something I've never told you."

"What?"

"For all the years we've known each other, I've been lying to you," Mia answered.

"Great." Jordan pursed his lips. "*Now* I find out my best friend is a liar?"

CHAPTER FIFTEEN

"You've got some nerve, Mia. Your boyfriend has accused me of crazy things and here you sit so cute and innocent with the biggest secret of all! What is it, by the way?" Jordan tapped the table.

"I come from a rich family," Mia confessed.

Jordan blinked and raised his brows. "You. Are. Rich."

"Not me personally, but my family is."

"You could ask them for money. Am I correct?" Jordan stared at her.

"Not always. When I started design school, they didn't support my dream. For the first time in my life, I defied their wishes and plans for my future. I had to support myself and pay for school."

"That part is true? When we first met you were a struggling artist like me?"

"Yes." Mia played with her fork, sticking it into the cake and removing tiny pieces. "My work ethic impressed my parents." She lifted her shoulder and chuckled. "My designs? Not so much. They saw I would not give up and offered to pay for the rest of my schooling. Once they saw my success at school, that someone else praised my designs, they wanted to invest in my future. By then I was used to being on my own. I liked depending on myself. No one looked at me and thought, 'There's the little rich girl. Everything is handed to her.' I had friends who liked me for me. So I declined their offer."

"I wouldn't have thought differently of you," Jordan said in a serious tone.

"You say that now, but who knows?" Mia paused. "You're not mad, are you? When times got tough for us, I could have asked my parents…"

Jordan held up his hand. "Stop. Say no more. I'm not mad and I don't blame you. Besides, I'm the one who found our backer. I'm proud I did it on my own with no help. Well, except for you."

Mia reached across the table. "Thank you, Jordan. As the years went by, it became harder and harder to tell you."

"At least I know why Rafe is after you. He discovered who you were." Jordan took in a breath, then exhaled slowly. "I see now why Kade is overprotective. I never liked Rafe. He always had a hungry look in his eye. Like he was after something."

"Me?" Mia joked, although she didn't find it funny.

"No. Something sinister." Jordan grimaced. "This is starting to make sense. I heard the word 'San Francisco' and 'job' a lot while I was at Miller Tech. If I'm correct, Rafe went to California as part of his job. While there, he did some investigating. He wanted to learn more about you and your family. You said you saw him at The Pearl. How did he know you'd be there?"

"I may have mentioned my uncle's memorial to him in passing. I don't quite remember." Mia shook her head. "In full disclosure, The Pearl was my uncle's hotel. Now his sons, my second cousins, run it."

"Wow! This keeps getting better and better. Rafe knew your family owned the hotel when you saw him this weekend."

"Yes," Mia answered. "Why would he think I'd take him back then? I'm not stupid. I'd know he was only interested in the money."

"Because the man never takes no for an answer. He gets what he wants or pulls a con to get it."

Mia widened her eyes. She hadn't thought of what Rafe might do since she blew him off. "Since I refused his offer, will Rafe pull a con?"

"On you? Yes, a tasteful one. One he hopes you don't see coming."

"You're scaring me, Jordan." *And making me even more determined to stop him and get him out of my life.*

"Jordan!" Annie called to him. "We're getting customers."

"Be right there, Annie," Jordan took Mia's hand. "Promise me you won't move. Once you had your quiet time, call Damien, and go back to Kade's. I'll let you know when I'm home." He slid back the chair, gave her one more threatening look and went behind the counter.

Mia ate her cake and sipped coffee, hoping Jordan would stop checking on her every fifteen seconds. Every time she looked toward the counter, his eyes met hers. She smiled and held up her cup in solidarity.

Mia glanced down at her tablet, but her mind went everywhere except fashion. She couldn't stop thinking about what Jordan said. *Is Kade secretly working for this agency? Is he some type of James Bond?* Mia mentally pictured him in a tuxedo with a martini in hand. *I could go for that.* She daydreamed about what she'd do to the man, then snapped herself back to reality. *I need to get out of here without Jordan noticing.*

Mia planned to walk to Town Hall, order takeout and wait in the bar until it was ready. She wanted him to see her. *I'm back, Rafe. If you want to try something, be my guest. Then I'll have your ass arrested for harassing me.* She cocked her head. *Is that possible?*

Out of the corner of her eye, Mia spotted Annie directing Jordan to the back of the shop. He appeared to argue his case to remain upfront, gesturing to someone else who could do the task. Annie's shoulders slumped, and she held up her pointer finger. *Does that mean just this once? Argh. I'll never escape.*

As the evening continued, the line grew longer, blocking Jordan's view. Mia slipped her tablet into her bag and dipped her head down to stay low after leaving the table. She tiptoed toward the door just as someone was coming in. He held the door for her and nodded. "Evening."

"Thanks," Mia responded and rushed down the sidewalk. *I made it!* She quickened her pace and arrived at Town Hall in record time. The takeout line was long, yet Mia didn't mind. *More time for Rafe to see me.*

To pass the time, Mia played with her phone, oblivious to her surroundings. Someone's breath on her neck startled her. "What do you think you're doing?" a voice asked.

"Jordan!" Mia spun in place. "You scared me half to death."

"Well, I'll take the other half." Jordan glared at her.

"I was hungry. I wanted an impossible burger."

"I do, too. I'll wait with you."

"Don't you have to work?"

"I asked Annie for an early break. We'll eat back at the shop in case she needs me."

You ruined my plan! Mia folded her arms as they waited in silence.

Burgers in hand, Jordan and Mia walked back to the coffee shop. "Are you ready to tell me the truth?" he asked. "You were looking for Rafe."

"I wanted a burger."

"What if he saw you and dragged you from the place? We'd have no idea where you were. Did you ever think of that?"

"No." Mia hung her head. "Sorry. I'll eat my burger and go home."

"Only if I walk you there, and you lock yourself in. Don't answer the door. What will you tell Kade?"

"I'll send him a text. Say I'm tired."

Jordan held to his promise. He saw Mia home, waited for her to get inside, and jiggled the front door of the building to make sure it was secure. She waved from the steps, hoping he'd get back to work without getting in trouble since he'd already taken a break. Mia convinced him to only walk her to the front door of the building to save time.

"Call me when you're in the apartment," Jordan had told her in a dad-like voice. "And don't open it for any reason."

* * * *

Kade received a text from Mia, saying she felt tired and planned to go home. "No! No! No! Does she ever listen?" He rushed to his bedroom, grabbed his wallet and sent Damien a message to come get him ASAP.

Ten minutes later, as he readied to leave, he got a text from Jordan. "Captain, I walked Mia home. She wouldn't let me take her up to the apartment. I watched her go up the steps and secured the front door. Then I looked around the building and went back to work. Highly suggest you check on her."

"Oh, I'm checking on her. Trust me. Where is Damien?" Having already texted him twice, Kade headed for the elevator to wait outside. "Why, Mia? You're making yourself a target. This isn't high school or college. Rafe's dangerous. You don't know who you're dealing with."

Beau and Kade had drawn the same conclusion. Rafe Salvadore had ties to the grifter community. His movements around the country and personality traits fit the lifestyle. Beau begged Kade to tread carefully. He felt Rafe wasn't a simple con artist. Beau thought his roots went deeper and even tried to link him to Gabe's old girlfriend, Blair Winters, and her father with no success.

A black Mercedes swerved into a parking space near the building. Damien's hand shot out of the driver's side window, waving to Kade. Kade jogged to the spot, hopped in the passenger side and said, "Floor it."

"It's Ms. Takeda, right? I hung out in that part of town waiting to hear from her. I never did. That's why it took me so long to get here."

"You did the right thing, Damien." Kade stared straight ahead, willing every light to remain green and every asshole driver to get out of the way.

"Are we going to the apartment or coffee shop?"

"Apartment."

"I don't know all the details, but I remember the guy standing in the shadows the first night I took Ms. Takeda home. I got out of the car and scared him off. It's got something to do with him. Am I right?"

"You are right, Damien, so right."

* * * *

Key in hand, Mia turned from the steps to walk down the third-floor hallway. Her breath hitched when she saw Rafe leaning against the wall next to her apartment door. "Rafe," she said under her breath.

Frozen to the floor, she willed herself to run. It felt like a bad dream. She couldn't move.

Rafe glanced up from his phone when he detected movement. "Mia! Hey, don't look so frightened. I dropped by to see you. You weren't home, so I thought I'd wait."

"How ... how did you get in?" Mia's teeth chattered.

"People are friendly. When I said I was your boyfriend and wanted to surprise you, some sweet old lady let me follow her in."

"Boyfriend?"

"Well, ex, but she probably wouldn't have bought that and let me in." Rafe chuckled. "Mia, my little butterfly, come here. I don't bite. You're acting like I'm the big bad wolf."

Maybe you are. Mia always loved when Rafe called her his little butterfly, but now it made her stomach churn. "What do you want?"

Three large strides and Rafe could grab her. She searched for an easy getaway. As her eyes darted around the area, something attracted her attention. Under her apartment door, a partial piece of paper stuck out. *Evidence! I caught Rafe in the act. I can stop him now. Get your act together. Stop being scared.* "Um." She looked down. "Something's under my door. Did you put it there?"

"Yes, I did."

"Like the others?"

Rafe wrinkled his brow. "I don't understand."

"You put two threatening letters under my door, Rafe. This is the third. I know why you did it."

"Please, enlighten me."

Mia wanted to smack the smug look off his face. "The first one said to leave and not come back. It had a picture of a gun under the words. You wanted me to go to San Francisco, hoping to win me back."

Rafe smiled. "If you ask me, that sounds quite romantic."

"Not when you're doing it for money. Let's get real. You discovered who I was and set this plan into motion." *Get him to confess.* "You wanted me somewhere you might have the upper hand. Funny. You never should have chosen The Pearl as the place to confront me."

"Hey, I loved you before I knew any of that. I tried to explain when I saw you at the hotel. My company sent me to California last minute. I'd put in for a transfer before I met you and it came up last minute. Damn it, Mia, I didn't want to go. While I was away, I could only think of you. You probably hated me for taking off and a text would never work. So, I requested a reassignment for the next quarter. I wanted to come back here for you. Explain everything."

Well played. "How did you know I'd be at The Pearl?"

"Your uncle was important to you, like a grandfather. See? I listen. I remember. Since I was in San Francisco, I visited the place. The employees were extremely helpful, especially when I mentioned I was a friend of the family."

"That's how you knew about the ceremony details."

"I was certain you'd come." Rafe took a step closer.

"Stay right there." Mia held out her arm, palm up.

"Fine." Rafe held his hands up in surrender. "Ask me anything. What do you want to know?"

"When I came home, there was another note shoved under the door." Mia's eyes flicked towards the floor. "It said I shouldn't have come back."

"I never would write that!" Rafe ran his hand through his hair. "I wanted you to come back so I could ask for a second chance."

"Rafe! Do you think I'm stupid?" Mia yelled. "You met me, researched my family and discovered you hit the jackpot. How many women have you done this to?"

"What?" Rafe looked as if Mia had struck him. "None. Never. You're it, butterfly. You and me. We were good together."

"Oh, yeah?" A voice came from the stairs.

Mia spun in place to see Kade behind her. In a protective gesture, he placed his hands on her shoulders and pulled her against his chest, then asked Rafe, "How good?"

CHAPTER SIXTEEN

"Hey, dude, this doesn't concern you," Rafe said. "Hit the road."

"Did you hear that, Damien," Kade said over his shoulder. "The man said to leave."

"I *did* hear, and I don't think so," Damien answered.

"Kade." Mia stared up at him. "Look under my door. We caught him in the act. Rafe was leaving another letter." He had put his hands down, but when she started for the door, Kade reached out to hold her back.

"Let him pick it up." Kade nodded toward Rafe, then to the white piece of paper sticking out from underneath the door. "Put it in Mia's hand."

Rafe smirked, bent down and tugged at the note, fully exposing it. It appeared smaller than a folder piece of copy paper. Rafe took one tentative step, checking to see if it was all right with Kade. Kade dipped his head then watched Rafe place it in Mia's open palm. "Get back," Kade ordered.

"Fine." Rafe smiled.

"Kade." Mia held up the note. "This is a cocktail napkin."

"Maybe he didn't have time to go home and get a proper sheet of paper," Kade snarled. "Open it. Let's see what it says this time."

Mia unfolded the napkin until it was lying flat in her hand. A 'Town Hall' logo printed in one corner caught Kade's eye. Rafe had used a black marker to write the message.

"Will you marry me?" Mia read in almost a whisper.

"Tell me?" Rafe asked, flinging his arms out from his sides. "What did I do that was so terrible?" His voice had grown louder with each word. "I saw Mia at Town Hall tonight. I was in the bar. The perfect idea came to me. She loves Town Hall. I grabbed a napkin, asked the bartender for a pen and wrote the message."

"The bartender will back up your story?" Kade growled.

"Yeah. Sure. Go ask her. I was in a hurry. I can't give you a detailed description. Blonde? About this high." Rafe lifted his hand to his shoulder. He looked at Mia with pleading eyes. "Will you, Mia? Marry me?"

"Enough! Shut your mouth." Kade dug his phone out of his back pocket and hit the number for Beau. "Damien, you stay with Mia. I'll be right over there." He walked back to the top of the staircase, waiting for Beau to answer.

"Kade?" Hearing Beau's voice calmed the anger growing inside him.

"Yeah, it's me. I'm here with Mia, Damien and Rafe."

"You caught him?"

"Not exactly. Let me tell you what happened." Kade described the scene as quickly as possible. When he finished, he waited for Beau's assessment of the situation.

"You're sure someone let him in."

"Yes. When we were coming up the stairs, I heard most of the conversation. Some lady let him in."

"Was he ever in the apartment?"

"No."

"The message written on the napkin said, 'Will you marry me?'"

"Yep."

"Sorry, bro, I got nothing." Beau sighed. "He didn't break any laws. The only thing you can do is threaten him with a restraining order. I can get it started."

"Let me talk to Mia first. I don't want to do anything without her okay."

"Sure. Text me whenever."

Kade hung up and returned to the hallway where the others stood silently.

"Well?" Rafe held up his hands and lifted his shoulders. "Are you going to arrest me? Did you call the police?"

"No, you can go. But, know this, Mia will file a restraining order against you in the morning." Kade glanced at her. "If you want."

Mia nodded. "I do."

"Damien will escort you out, *Mr.* Salvadore," Kade said in a sarcastic tone.

"I know the way out." Rafe winked. "I don't need someone to show me. Mia, think about it. Him or me? I'm only a phone call away."

Rafe passed them by and Kade felt every muscle in his body tense. He yearned to punch the man's lights out and beat him until the smirk left his face. Mia's hand wrapped around his arm and she lightly squeezed. "I can see the twitch of your jaw. Please calm down. I'm sorry I put you in this position."

"Don't be sorry," Kade said and placed his arm across her shoulders. "Let's go inside, shall we?"

"What about Damien?"

"He'll make sure Rafe leaves," Kade replied.

"Will you stay until Jordan gets home?" Mia's voice quivered.

"I will stay as long as you want," Kade answered. "I'll sleep on the couch and we'll go to Beau's first thing in the morning." He took Mia into his arms and brushed his lips against hers. "Everything will look better in the morning."

* * * *

Kade was right. Things do look better in the morning light. Mia quickly showered and dressed before checking on him. She found him in the kitchen making coffee. "Sleep well?" Kade asked as he searched the cupboards.

"Yes," Mia answered. "Looking for mugs? You want the cupboard to your left."

"Thanks." Kade chuckled, found the cups and turned to her. "A restraining order is all we can do for now. Hope you're okay with it."

"I am." Mia slid her arms around Kade's waist. "I think he got the message. I'm with you. He is ancient history." She dropped her arms and took the mugs from him. "We only dated for three months. I met him over the Christmas holidays. Everything was fun and festive. Maybe that's why I fell for him. Obviously, I was more invested in the relationship than Rafe. He hurt me when he disappeared without so much as a call or text. I've wondered if I would have taken him back if not for you."

"I'm glad I came along when I did." Kade checked the coffee setting, then pulled her toward him. "I'd die before I let anything happen to you."

"Don't say that. Rafe's not a serial killer or a rapist. Let's keep it in perspective. In fact, I have an idea."

"Ooh, when Mia gets an idea, watch out," Jordan called from the bedroom hallway. He walked into the kitchen wearing only his boxers. "I smell coffee."

"How about if you get dressed?" Kade chided him. "I ordered some breakfast sandwiches. They should be here soon."

"Aye, aye, Captain." Jordan rolled his eyes as he walked past Mia. "While you're at it, why don't you get us some air conditioning?" he called as he disappeared down the hall. "Then I wouldn't walk around like this."

"Very funny, Jordan," Mia said. "Hurry. I want to tell you my plan."

"We need to discuss today's schedule, too." Kade checked his phone. "Looks like we have a delivery. Breakfast is here. I'll get it."

Mia settled in at the dinette table to wait. If someone had told her that her life would drastically change within a week's time, she would have thought they were playing with her. Yet it had. She finally felt like a real fashion designer, met the man she wanted to spend her life with and found out Rafe Salvadore was a con man. In her heart, she didn't want to acknowledge the accusations against him. Her head told her something different. *Believe it.*

Kade wrapped on the door. "I'm back, Mia."

"Hmm, should I let you in?" Mia teased as she approached the entryway. "You could be disguising your voice."

"Very funny."

Mia opened the door to find Kade holding up the bag of breakfast sandwiches. "I'll eat them out here if you don't let me in."

"Very funny." Mia repeated his line. "Get in here." She laughed.

Jordan sat at the table as if he'd magically appeared. "You weren't here a minute ago," Mia said.

"When I heard the food was here, I came out. You didn't see me?" His eyes twinkled with mischief. She had her old Jordan back.

Kade hadn't trusted Jordan, and for a moment she doubted him, too. Relieved it was in the past, she hoped they'd all become friends. Mia loved the banter between them. It felt normal and natural. She wished the wonderful moment could last yet knew better. They needed to have a serious discussion about Rafe, and she didn't want to waste a minute.

"Guys." Mia looked at Kade, then Jordan. "I want the three of us to go to Town Hall tonight."

"Absolutely not," Kade growled.

"Let me finish, Kade." Mia stared at him. "Hopefully, I'll have the restraining order by then. Will I?"

"You should." Kade nodded.

"Rafe will most likely be there. I want him to see I'm not afraid of returning to the restaurant or the bar. If he approaches, I'll present the paperwork. I want this to end tonight. Are you with me?"

"I'm in," Jordan said. "It makes sense. Rafe will know to stay away. We can call the police if he doesn't."

"I agree with the logic," Kade stated. "I wish we had more on him."

"Well, we don't," Mia said. "But I want to put this behind me. We have important work to do at the loft. The show is only weeks away."

"Speaking of the show, Yani texted me," Jordan said. "He said to expect a surprise when we get to the loft."

"Ooh, that sounds like good news." Mia tingled with anticipation. "We're stopping at Miller Tech before the loft, Jordan. I hope you can wait. I don't know if I can." She rubbed her hands together. "This is real, isn't it?"

"Yup." Jordan nodded. "As real as it will ever get."

* * * *

"Oh. My. Gosh." Mia grabbed Jordan's hand. "Did we really design this?"

A mannequin wore a mockup of one of their designs. Shiny, straight pins held the material in place. The dress needed some final touches, yet it looked like a completed product.

"Yani wasn't kidding when he said he had a surprise for us." Jordan held up their intertwined hands as if they'd won a competition. "Am I dreaming?"

"No," Kade placed one hand on Mia's shoulder, the other on Jordan's. "You're not."

"When will they get here? I can't wait to hug and kiss them," Mia said.

"Yani texted me last night and asked if they could stay late. Since I was at your apartment, I told them they could have the place to themselves for the night. I see they took advantage of the time but it looks like there's more work to do. I bet they went home to get some sleep before coming back here."

"No, we didn't." Yani strolled from Kade's bedroom. "You love?" He pointed to the outfit, then narrowed his eyes when he looked at Kade. "You did say we could stay."

"We? Who else is in there?" Kade rubbed his chin and chuckled as three more people appeared.

"It was one big lovefest." Yani joked and hugged Hope, one of the seamstresses. "Right, babe?"

Hope laughed and winked at Kade, shaking her head.

"Your bed is wonderful," Chelsea said as she ran a finger along Kade's back.

"You might not want to go in there," Violet teased. "Give me the number to your cleaning service. I'll arrange a time for them to come today."

"All right enough." Kade laughed. "You guys are doing an outstanding job. And, Violet, don't worry, the service is coming today."

Kade stood back and watched the team interact with Jordan and Mia. The look on Mia's face was priceless. Kade snapped a few pictures without them knowing. Mia might enjoy seeing them later. He pointed his camera at the mannequin, wearing a flowing summer midi dress, and took more. After he finished, Kade thought he'd give the designers some space, leave the loft and call Smith as he walked the streets of Soho. He wanted to hear it straight from the man's mouth. This had to be the end of his mission or so he hoped.

"Mia," Kade approached her and whispered in her ear. "I've got some business to conduct. I'm going outside. Remember, I'm only a text or phone call away."

"Kade." Mia slipped her hand into his. "This is unbelievable. Thank you."

"You did all the work," he replied, then snuck a kiss. "I won't be gone long. An hour or two." Kade made eye contact with Jordan and nodded. He appeared to catch the meaning. Watch over Mia.

Once out on the street, Kade took notice of the beautiful day. Some humidity had left the air, making it a good time to walk. He slipped on his aviators and dialed Smith.

"Mr. Phillips." Smith's voice held a touch of surprise. "I did not think I would hear from you again."

"I'm checking in, Smith. I want to make sure my mission is complete before I see the guys on Friday."

"Have you handled Mr. Salvadore?"

"To the best of my ability. Mia has a restraining order. It's the best we could do. We caught him in her apartment building last night, but someone let him inside. He'd slipped a note under her door, but it was not like the others. It said, 'Will you marry me?' We can't arrest him for that."

"No, you cannot. Is Ms. Takeda satisfied with the outcome?"

"Yes. In fact, she's at my loft right now. The team surprised her and Jordan with a partially finished dress. I snapped a few pictures."

"That was thoughtful of you. You did well, Mr. Phillips. Your assignment was the most complicated of all. I had no idea what Mr. Salvadore would do. You will continue to watch over Ms. Takeda?"

"With my life." Kade breathed a sigh of relief. *I'm done. I saved the Society's money, yet I got so much more.*

"Quite a statement. You must care for the girl."

"You mean woman? And yes, I do."

CHAPTER SEVENTEEN

Town Hall was its usual crowded and noisy self. Mia followed Kade and Jordan up to the bar to order drinks and get a better look around. Across the way, in his usual spot, Rafe leaned against the bar. His back was to them and he laughed and gestured as if in an animated conversation. Mia watched his head bob up and down. The hand which held a beer bottle was used to make a point. His shoulders jiggled as if he heard a good joke. *Who is he with?* His frame blocked her view.

Rafe turned to place the bottle on the bar and ordered another. Mia couldn't keep her eyes from him, wanting him to notice her. When he finally did, he raised his eyebrows and tipped the bottle in her direction. Before he could look away, she held up the documents for him to see. He lifted a shoulder and one corner of his mouth.

"He doesn't seem too upset," Jordan whispered in her ear. "It also looks like he's hooking up with someone. Wow. He moved on fast."

The comment stung, yet Jordan was right. Everything Rafe did with Mia and said last night, meant nothing. "Can you see who he's talking to?" Mia asked.

"No, but I will before the night's over."

"Let's sit over there," Kade said. "I want to see if he tries anything. He might not know you held up a restraining order, Mia."

"Look like you're having a good time." Jordan poked her. "Your face is giving you away, like you want to kill the guy."

"I've done nothing like this before." Mia defended herself. "Kade, do I look too serious?"

"Well…" Kade played with his drink, bourbon on the rocks, rolling the ice cubes around the glass.

"Hey," Mia said as she settled in his lap. "Is this better?"

"Much." Kade tugged her close. "If it would make you feel better, I'll take the doc over there and show it to him."

"No, he's not stupid. I think he got the message."

"Fine. Then our work here is done." Kade nuzzled her neck. "I can't wait until Saturday," he whispered in her ear.

"Ooh, what's happening on Saturday?" Jordan asked, putting his elbows on the table and resting his head on his hands.

"How did you hear that?" Mia glared at him in a teasing way. "I swear you have bionic hearing."

"I do. You know that. So are you going to tell me?"

"It's between me and Kade. But if you must know … Ooh!" Mia jumped when Kade nudged her. "Kade and I are going out for a special dinner."

"That's it? Boring." Jordan leaned against his chair. "Wait!" He held up his pointer finger. "It's not just dinner, right? It's what will happen after." He smiled. "About time."

"We should have our drawings completed by Thursday. Friday the latest. I wanted to celebrate," Mia replied. "That's all."

"And so did I," Kade added.

"If you won't tell me. Fine. But…" Jordan straightened his body and his eyes darted toward the bar. "Guys! I can see who's with Rafe. You'll never guess who it is." His face said it all. Whatever he saw shocked him. "Poppy!"

"What?" Mia strained to see.

"Is she aware you dated him, Mia?" Kade asked.

"No."

"Somehow he discovered you two are friends." Kade shifted Mia on his lap to get a better look. "You said he was here the day you saw Poppy and Mason for the first time. He's observant. I'm sure he committed them to memory."

"As any good con artist should do," Mia said, hoping it sounded like a joke.

"They're leaving!" Jordan said in a loud whisper. "Together!"

* * * *

Mia and Jordan rose early the next morning to get to the loft in record time. Determined to finish their sketches by Friday, they wanted to get to work ASAP. Soon after they arrived, Jordan's phone made a noise indicating he had a text. "Mia, come here." He motioned to her. "Mason sent me a message. Read this."

Mia slid from her stool, walked to his desk and read over his shoulder. "Got this text from Poppy this morning. It sounds rather cryptic. What do you think? Is she all right?" Mia squeezed Jordan's shoulder. "I don't know what to think. Let me get Kade."

Kade tried to give them space while they worked, but Mia never considered him in the way. She went to the kitchen where Kade sat at the island, reading something on his phone. "Kade, could you…"

"I'm right behind you, Mia," Jordan interrupted. He handed his cell to Kade. "We need your opinion."

They waited while he silently read the message. Mia stared at Jordan and repeated the rest of Poppy's message. "She told Mason, 'I'm fine. Don't look for me.' That's all she said? You need to ask him."

"Does Poppy live with Mason?" Kade looked up from Jordan's phone.

"No," Mia answered. "She's got a cute studio over a consignment shop in the Village."

"They hook up," Jordan added. "I don't think it's serious."

Kade wrinkled his brow. "It must be more than they're letting on. She's assuming he'd worry or go looking for her if she weren't around."

"He might." Jordan shrugged. "I don't keep track of their love life."

"They may have gotten serious since they've been in New York, Jordan. You said you saw them together at Town Hall this weekend." Mia hoped to jar his memory.

"True. But I thought they'd come separately."

"Any signs of affection? Hand holding? Did they leave together?" Kade asked.

"Maybe?" Jordan rubbed his temple.

"You are terrible at this," Mia said. "Here's my theory. I think they are at the beginning of a relationship. Poppy cheats on him with Rafe. She stayed overnight and didn't want Mason looking for her in the usual places, so she sent the message."

"Like the coffee shop," Jordan said with excitement. "I just thought of something. She comes in every morning. At least on the days I'm there."

"Which means every day. You go there whether or not you work." Mia teased.

"Does she meet Mason at the coffee shop?" Kade demanded. His frustration made Mia want to giggle. He'd soon learn Jordan ignored other relationships unless it was hers.

"Yeah, some days he does." Jordan wiped his face, then added. "I think." He rolled his eyes and blew through his lips. "Are we done with the inquisition? I'm starting to sweat."

Mia's phone pinged. "Saved by the bell." She glanced at the screen. "Ugh. I need to change my number. I got a text from Rafe. Delete."

"No, stop! You need to read it," Kade said. "And you're right. We must get you a new number."

Mia nodded. She opened the text and gasped.

"What?" both Jordan and Kade yelled.

"It's …. it's Poppy." Mia turned her phone so they could see the screen. Rafe had handcuffed Poppy to a bed still wearing the outfit she'd worn last night.

"Everyone does that." Jordan waved his hand.

"Not fully dressed." Mia's hand shook. *Did Rafe ever want to do that to me but was afraid I was too prim and proper?* "Besides, he never…"

"Don't say it." Kade held his hand up. "Too much information."

"Kade." Mia placed a hand on her hip. "I wanted to say he never suggested something like that."

"He may have thought you weren't that kind of girl, Mee." Jordan lifted his brows, confirming what she'd thought. "But Poppy?"

"Are you inferring I'm boring?" Mia narrowed her eyes at him.

"Okay, you two. Stop. Let's get back to the picture. It might be sexual or Rafe's sending you a message. I think he wants you to know he has Poppy."

"Or," Jordan said. "It *is* sexual and Rafe is sending you the picture to make you jealous."

"That makes no sense, Jordan. Poppy wouldn't agree to pose for a picture so Rafe could send it to an ex." Mia ran a hand through her hair. "Kade's right. He wants me to know he has Poppy. The bastard! He's in control again."

"Everyone," Kade said. "Let's take a breath. Mia, may I send the picture to Beau?"

"Yes." Mia texted the picture to Kade's phone.

"He'll analyze her expression and body position. Maybe he'll pick up something in the background that will tell us where they are."

Tears filled Mia's eyes. "Whatever he's doing, he's using her. Poor Poppy. She's my friend. You'll help her, Kade, right?'

"Whatever the circumstance, yes." Kade bobbed his head once.

"I think we've boiled it down to two options," Jordan said. "Sexual or he's holding her hostage."

"There's one more," Kade replied. "He's playing with us."

"Which one is it?" Mia cried. Her world was crumbling around her. She'd been so happy yesterday, and now Rafe had thrown another bomb into her life, trying to blow it up. Her phone pinged again. "It's from Rafe!"

Kade rushed to her side and pulled her close. "We'll read it together."

"Read it aloud so I can hear," Jordan said.

Mia opened the message and recited the text. "Should I keep her or let her go?" She collapsed against Kade and his strong arms went around her. "That sounds so creepy! This is all my fault," she sobbed.

"It's not," Kade whispered, rubbing her back.

"Poppy's in trouble." Mia sniffed. "And it's not my fault? I think it is."

"Mee," Jordan said. "Poppy didn't have to leave the bar with him. It was her choice. If she stayed, she wouldn't be a hostage right now."

"You think she's a hostage?" Mia widened her eyes and a fresh set of tears flowed.

"Sorry." Jordan hung his head. "She may not be a hostage, just having a good time."

"If she is being kept against her will," Mia looked to Kade. "What does he want? This is definitely not the way to win me back."

"Rafe realizes you won't come back to him, Mia," Kade said. "It's all about the money now. Prepare yourself. He may ask for a ransom." He took her by the shoulders. "Look. The design team should arrive any minute. You two need to act like nothing is wrong. I'm going to Miller Tech. I'll call you if we discover anything."

* * * *

"Remember Tess' ex?" Beau asked as he and Kade headed to his office. "I couldn't pin much on him and if I found something, Tess would never let me go through with it."

"Weren't his parents rich?"

"Yeah, they added to the problem. If we'd arrested him, I'm sure they would have bailed him out and covered up her abduction."

"We've learned a lot from these missions, haven't we?" Kade shook his head. "People are never who you think they are."

"Like Smith?" Beau joked.

"Exactly." Kade chuckled. "How is Tess? Is she here? I'd love to meet her."

"She drives into Jersey City each workday. Tess and her sister Sherri have a small cyber security business there. If you remember, that was my assignment."

"To help them?"

"Yes." Beau paused. "Her sister was sabotaging her own business. Sherri felt overwhelmed at the time and did something stupid instead of asking for help. Tess forgave her. I wish she'd work from here. I even offered to move The Roberts Group to this building and have it become part of us. They politely declined. I don't think Sherri's heart is in the business anymore. Tess is loyal though. She won't give up until her sister does."

"Was Tess' ex part of your assignment?" Kade asked.

"No, he was an added bonus." Beau smirked. "But I got the girl. Just like in the movies."

"You're such a movie buff." Kade smiled. "You even waited for Tess and her answer at the top of the Empire State building. Straight out of the movies."

"Hey, don't slam a guy for trying." Beau held out his arms. "It worked, didn't it? She forgave me for lying to her and we became a couple."

"You didn't lie, Beau. Smith *made* you lie. There's a difference." Kade and his buddies liked to blame Smith for their recent troubles. But it was true, he'd gotten them into a lot of messes, and they had to dig themselves out without his help. *Am I being too hard on him? Smith comes through in the end.*

Still, something gnawed at Kade and he wanted Beau's opinion. "Do you think Rafe was my mission?"

"Yes, I do. Protecting Mia was a part of it, too. I haven't figured out the connection between all of them yet, but I will."

"Since I took care of Rafe to the best of my abilities and Mia is safe, I'm done. I completed the mission, right?"

"Why all the doubts, Kade?" Beau gave him a troubled look. "You're like a dog with a bone. You won't let this go."

"I haven't heard Smith say the words. I want to hear, 'Yes, you've completed the mission.' He's implied I am done yet doesn't confirm it. I'm the last one. I need to know I saved us."

"Hey, don't be so hard on yourself. You did what he asked. You finished your assignment."

"Easy for you to say."

"Beau!" Blake, Beau's brother, half ran, half slid into the room. "Oh, hi, Kade. Didn't see you there."

"Blake." Kade nodded. "Got something for us?"

"Yes, I'm glad you're here." Blake set a picture in front of Beau and handed him a magnifying glass. "You can make out the last two letters of the storefront through the window." He turned to Kade. "There's a piece of a window in the shot you sent. We've blown it up as much as we could without distorting it." He looked at Beau. "I sent it to Tess, as you requested, and she identified the shop."

"Excellent work." Beau studied the picture with the magnifying glass.

"There are four stores in the city. We checked each one. Only two are close to hotels. We couldn't find any nearby apartments."

Beau glanced up. "What do you think, Kade? We haven't seen the guy go near his apartment. He took her to a hotel?"

"It makes sense. Which one is closer to the Village?" Kade asked. "Give me the address and I'm out of here."

"Hold on." Beau pushed his chair back and stood. "Not without me. Did Damien drive you here?"

"Yeah, he's waiting in your employee lounge."

"Great. Let him know we're coming."

On the way down to the first floor, Kade called Mia.

"Hello?" Mia sounded tentative. "Please tell me you've got something."

"We hope so."

"Pick me up on your way."

"Nope. Beau and I are handling this."

"Please," Mia begged.

"I promise to keep you informed, Mia. It's the best I can do."

"Fine." Mia sighed. "Let me know as soon as Poppy's safe."

"I will. See you soon." Kade had a sudden urge to say, "I love you". *Too soon.*

They walked to the parking garage where Damien stood next to the car. "You got a lead?" he asked Kade.

"Yes." Kade placed a piece of paper in Damien's hand. "Here's the address."

Only one hotel fit the profile. Beau and Kade planned for Damien to drop them a block away while he circled the block. They'd approach the building calmly, as if they had rooms there. It was getting close to checkout time. If he'd only booked one night, Rafe would have to checkout, forcing him to leave the room.

They planned for Kade to sit in the lobby while Beau used his skills as a security master to get information about Rafe Salvadore. Kade would watch the bank of elevators until Beau returned from his inquiry.

"Act casual," Beau said under his breath. "You look too driven. Like an animal zoned in on its prey."

"I *am* stalking my prey." Kade grasped Beau's upper arm to slow him. "Hold on." He blinked to make sure it wasn't a vision. "I swear that's Poppy."

"You mean the woman with the bedraggled ponytail sliding down one side of her head and still wearing the clothes she'd wear to a club?" Beau asked.

"Yes, that's her. Do you think she escaped?" Kade asked. Poppy kept looking over her shoulder as she walked away from the hotel. "She looks nervous."

"Let's find out."

Poppy stopped and dug in her handbag, making their approach easier.

"Poppy?" Kade pointed at her. "Mia's friend."

"Oh. My. God. No." Poppy looked up after finding her sunglasses. Black mascara or eyeliner, Kade didn't know which, had made smudges below her eyes and onto her cheeks.

"Are you all right?"

"Yes. No! You caught me in my walk of shame!" Poppy glared at him. "I didn't want anyone to find out."

"You're free to do as you choose. You're not engaged or married, are you?" Kade grinned. "Walk of shame, huh?"

Poppy came closer to him. "Between you and me? I met this handsome guy at the Hall last night. He asked me to spend the night. I had a little too much to drink and voila!" She swung her arm towards the hotel. "I end up here."

"Since you're a friend of Mia's, I have to ask. Are you okay?" Kade tapped below his eyes.

"That?" Poppy shrugged. "Makeup." She slipped on the sunglasses.

"He didn't hurt you or threaten you? Because I got a guy here." Kade gestured to Beau. "Who's in the security business."

"What? No. Besides the handcuffs, he was a perfect gentleman."

"Handcuffs, eh?" Kade chuckled but inwardly wanted to find Rafe and tell him to stop this shit with a punch or two thrown in for good measure.

"Fully clothed," Poppy said out of the side of her mouth as she placed her hand next to it. "Not very sensual. I don't know what he was thinking. But later?"

"Okay, enough." *I think she's still drunk.* "You may regret you told me as much as you did." Kade hoped he'd said it in a light, joking way, then looked at Beau. "We better go."

"Do you need a ride home, ma'am?" Beau asked.

"Ooh, such the gentleman. Are you part of the ride package?" Poppy cooed.

"No, but I've called a car for you. I hope you don't mind."

"Mind? Is it free?"

"Absolutely."

Impressed, Kade gave Beau a nod. When one of Beau's cars pulled up next to the curb, Kade made a note to ask how he'd pulled it off so fast, but that would have to wait. They still had a job to do. He wanted to go into the hotel and find good old Rafe Salvadore.

CHAPTER EIGHTEEN

"I hate to say it, Kade. The man did nothing wrong." Beau shook his head. "He's playing you. Hopefully, we can make him back off."

"We?"

"You didn't think I'd let you do this alone?" Beau gave him a look of surprise. "You haven't seen him come out of the hotel, have you?"

"No."

"Then we'll sit in the lobby and wait. Then let me have some fun with him."

Kade smiled and shook his head. "Have at it."

Half an hour later, Kade spotted Rafe coming from the bank of elevators. He nudged Beau to signal Rafe's arrival.

"I'm on it." Beau reached in his back pocket and pulled out a thin black leather wallet. He flipped back the top to expose a badge.

"Is that real?" Kade pointed to the silver emblem.

"As real as it gets. It's a Miller Tech security badge and difficult to come by. Do you know how many hours of training you need to put in to get one of these?" Beau grinned. "Wish me luck." He rose from the chair and looked back at Kade. "Nah, I'm fooling. I don't need luck."

Even though he wanted to jump up and follow Beau, Kade remained seated as promised. Every nerve stood on edge as he watched Beau approach Rafe.

Kade had texted Mia earlier and his phone showed he had a message from her. A good distraction. He glanced at the screen and read, "I am so glad she's safe! Thank you. What are you going to do about Rafe?"

Kade typed in, "Beau's taking care of him." He glanced up to see Rafe and Beau in a heated discussion.

"No matter how it looks, do *not* interfere." Beau had told him.

If he puts his hands on you, I will. Kade watched their every move until they parted ways. Beau stood with his hands on his hips and watched until Rafe was out of sight. Once he went through the front doors, Beau waved for Kade to join him. "Let Damien know we're ready," he said. "We'll speak in the car."

Kade's nerves were already on end. He wanted to know everything *now*, yet he did as Beau requested. He texted Damien and waited curbside until the car arrived. As soon as they were in the backseat, Kade turned to Beau. "What got him so angry? I thought he was going to punch you."

"I told him to tread carefully. As soon as he stepped outside the hotel, someone would watch his every move. Rafe said his civil rights were being violated, and I reminded him of Mia and the restraining order. One wrong move and I'd be all over him. He got the message, Kade. Don't worry. Mia won't hear from the bastard again. If he tries something, he's a fool."

"I can't thank you enough, Beau." Kade ran his hand through his hair. "I now know how you guys felt during your assignments. My brain is a jumbled mess. Sometimes I can't think straight."

"Welcome to the world of Smith's Mission Impossible." Beau chuckled. "Glad mine's behind me."

"Was it worth it, Beau?"

"I met Tess. You met Mia. So, yes," Beau acknowledged. "Strange how we all found someone, except for Nash. He already had his girl."

"If I remember correctly, they'd broken up."

"Now, because of Smith, they're back together."

"Mr. Miller, sir?" Damien glanced back at him after parking in front of the loft. "Would you like me to take you back to Miller Tech?"

"Yes, I would, Damien. Thank you." Beau turned to Kade. "See you on Friday?"

"Yep." Kade nodded. "I'll see you at the airport."

* * * *

Mia paced in front of the large front windows of the loft. Occasionally, she'd peek down at the street. "I can't stand this!"

"Hey," Jordan said. "You need to stop. The team is getting suspicious. Good thing they all went out for lunch because they were giving you odd looks all morning." He came and stood behind her. "Mia, you have nothing to worry about. Kade texted you. He said Poppy is safe. I can't wait to hear the actual story."

"Which I can tell you now." Kade's voice came from the foyer.

"Kade!" Mia rushed to him and threw her arms around him. "I've never been so worried in my life. If Rafe hurt you…"

"He didn't." Kade hugged her tightly. "Where is everyone?"

"It's a nice day, so they wanted to go out for lunch," Jordan answered. "I'm glad they did. Gives us time to talk." He gestured to the island where someone had placed trays of food for their lunch.

As they filled their plates, Kade described Poppy's walk of shame, Mia noticed Jordan trying hard not to laugh. He pressed his lips tightly together and widened his eyes. "Jordan," she scolded.

"Sorry, it's just that." Jordan lifted his hand. "I'd loved to have seen it."

"Poppy is fine?" Mia asked.

"A little embarrassed, but she's okay. Poppy never expected to see someone she knew," Kade replied with a smile. "Beau ordered a car to drive her home. Then we went inside to wait for Rafe. Beau spoke to him and we left."

"Spoke to him?" Mia questioned. "That's it?"

"He kept it low key, Mia. Beau let Rafe know someone is watching him. A true con artist would fold his cards and move on. Let's hope he does." Kade reached for Mia's hand. "Show me what you've worked on since I left."

Grateful the Rafe situation was finally over, Mia eagerly accepted his invitation. "When you get back on Saturday, Jordan and I will have a complete portfolio to show you," she said. "Come on. I can't wait to show you what we've done."

"Before you two lovebirds get all cozy over there, I'd like to talk," Jordan said.

"About what?" Mia tilted her head. "I thought everything was good."

"It is. Almost." Jordan stared at Kade. "I want to discuss the loft. You may have thought it was a joke, but I didn't."

"Oh." Kade nodded. "I've been thinking about it, too."

"You have?" Jordan's eyes lit with excitement.

"Here's the deal." Kade folded his arms. "I'll lease you a loft for a dollar a year for three years. Hopefully, you'll have made it big by then. You can continue to live there for full price thereafter or move on. That's my best offer." Kade tapped his chin. "With one amendment."

Jordan's shoulders slumped. "What?"

"You save your money during that time."

"That's it?" Jordan's face brightened.

"I'll need to see statements."

"Okay, I can do that." Jordan smiled at Mia. "We'll make the place our own."

"I don't know about Mia," Kade said. "She may not want to live with you."

"Why not?" Jordan asked.

Kade smiled at her. "She might get a better offer."

* * * *

Kade climbed the stairs of the plane to find Beau already seated. "It should be a smooth flight," the attendant told him.

"Thanks," Kade said. "Hey, Beau. How are you?"

"Good. Yourself?"

"My life has finally slowed to a normal pace. I can breathe easier now."

"Hmm." Beau rubbed his chin. "Seems like that happens after a mission is over."

"Do you think Smith will return our money today?"

Beau sat back in the cushioned leather seat and sighed. "That is the question of the day. If you ask me, I'd say no."

"What's your reason?" Kade felt confused. "Six assignments. Six completed. What else could he want?"

"Control."

Kade sprang to his feet. "What?"

"Please, Mr. Phillips, return to your seat." A voice came from the front of the plane. "Take off is in five minutes."

"Sorry," Kade said as he sat and buckled his seatbelt. "Beau, you son of a bitch, you better be wrong."

"What if I'm not?" Beau raised a brow.

"Then you know what will happen."

This time Beau looked confused. "No. What?"

"Everyone will look to you to fix this."

"Why?"

"You're the man, Beau. Everyone thinks Chase is the unofficial leader of the Society. Not me and Gabe." Kade shook his head. "It's you."

"Get out."

"Nope. I'm telling you the truth." Kade leaned forward. "Who did Nash turn to first when he needed help with his assignment? You."

"Sure he would. We're best friends. Besides, we all helped with that one."

"Okay, I'll give you that. But you stayed on to help find Vanessa. Let me ask you this. Who found Smith?"

"I did."

"Who's the only one helping me with my mission?"

"Me, but we're both in New York."

"Keep making excuses, Beau, but you know as well as I do, when the shit hits the fan, we turn to you. Cool, calm and collected Beau Miller."

After a smooth two-hour flight, the plane touched down at Chase's private airport in Charlotte, North Carolina. When they disembarked, Kade spotted the one person who'd understand his ordeal more than anyone. His buddy Gabe leaned on the hood of a limo and raised his hand once he realized Kade had seen him.

"Hey, man!" Kade slapped Gabe on the back when he reached his best friend. "Were you waiting for us?"

"Yeah, I hardly heard from you during your mission. I got a little worried. Seems like you had help." Gabe nodded toward Beau.

"Don't start," Kade said. "Beau runs a tech company in New York. Of course, I turned to him."

"Gabe!" Beau finally caught up to them.

"Beau, good to see you," Gabe said as they shook hands.

"Here's another one who confides in you," Kade said, pointing to Gabe.

"Cut it out, Kade," Beau smirked. "You'll give me a big head."

"Don't you already have one?" Kade smirked.

"Oh, it's on." Beau threw an air punch and Kade returned one. They laughed as they made their way to the car, joking and mock fighting. It was the most normal Kade had felt in weeks.

* * * *

Nash stood in the driveway as the limo pulled up to the garage and parking area. He waved in greeting. "Hard to believe this is our last meeting with Smith," Nash said to the group as they exited the limo.

"I'm so happy, I want to kiss him on the lips!" he joked, then grabbed Beau to demonstrate.

"Knock it off." Beau pushed Nash in the chest. "Although, I'm glad to see you're back to your juvenile ways."

"Hey, I take offense to that!" Nash chuckled. "Seriously, it took a while to get over what happened to Van. I couldn't let her out of my sight for days after we rescued her."

"I hear you." Beau slapped him on the shoulder. "After I found Tess, I felt the same way, too."

"Her ex took her to the family cabin," Nash replied. "Not some cartel who could have killed her."

"True." Beau looked at Kade and Gabe. "Shall we?"

The four guys walked through the kitchen, greeted Renata, Chase's house manager and Nash's soon to be mother-in-law, then continued out to the stone patio, which was more like an extension of the house. Chase and Finn sat at the long table, beers in hand.

"Grab a beer," Finn called to them. "And join us."

"We have no idea when Smith will call so we'll eat an early dinner," Chase said. "Renata insisted."

Kade hung back and waited for Gabe. After they chose their drinks from the outdoor fridge, he asked in a quiet voice, "Still planning to quit?"

"Yeah, but not tonight. Not really the time to do it. I'll see how this plays out." Gabe paused and stared at him. "How are *you*? You look like you could use a good night's sleep."

"That bad?" Kade smiled. "I tried to keep you updated, but it was hard. Something was always happening."

"From the messages you sent, it sounds like we have another con artist at large. At least, I caught mine." Gabe gave him a deadpan look, then grinned. "Not as easy as you thought, huh?"

"I'd love to have gotten him on some charge, Gabe. This guy is too slick."

"If you had Beau's help, that's all you could do. He has someone tailing the guy, right?"

"Yes, and Rafe knows it. I'm hoping he moves on to his next victim and leaves Mia alone … as crass as it sounds."

"I know what you mean." Gabe shook his head. "Who ever thought we'd deal with con artists?"

"Hey, girlfriends! What are you chattering about over there?" Nash yelled. "Get over here."

"Let's go," Kade said to Gabe. "Before Nash starts singing love songs."

During dinner, the guy's phones pinged, signaling the arrival of Mr. Smith. Kade's heartbeat sped up, and he broke into a sweat. *What if he says I didn't complete my mission? He implied I did but could tell the guys anything. I'd ruin it for everyone.*

"Kade," Gabe said, leaning toward him. "You look like you've seen a ghost."

"I hope not. I'm just worried. Does it show?"

"Not really. Remember, I've known you since we were ten. You're rubbing your palms together and running your hand through your hair. I know your tells."

"Once Smith announces I completed my mission, I'll be fine."

"Let's get it over with then." Gabe pushed his chair back. "I must admit I will miss the guy."

"Not me." Kade shook his head. "I had no idea what I was doing until Smith agreed Rafe was the target."

"Really?" Gabe widened his eyes. "Seems like Smith didn't have a clue and hoped you'd run into Rafe."

Kade pulled Gabe aside before going into the bunker. "See? You think like me. Remember my original mission? Move Jordan's fashion show to August. What did that have to do with Rafe Salvadore, the con artist?"

"Agree." Gabe nodded his head. "Why don't you ask him?" He pointed his thumb over his shoulder towards the interrogation room.

"Yeah, like he'd answer."

"So true." Gabe chuckled.

The six settled into the two rows of three seats. Finn, Nash and Chase chose the row behind Kade, Gabe and Beau. No one cracked a joke. They sat in eerie silence. Kade only heard his breathing and the inhale, exhale of the other five guys.

"Good evening, gentleman." Smith's voice came over the speaker. "You are all here."

"Where did he think we'd be?" Nash said under his breath.

Kade stood before anyone else spoke. "Tell them, Smith." The roar of blood rushing through his brain made him feel faint. His hand flew to his head, and he rubbed his forehead.

"Tell them what, Mr. Phillips?"

"I completed my mission."

"You did."

Relief spread through him, calming every nerve in his body. Kade sank into his seat. "Thank you," he whispered.

"Now," Smith said. "On to the business of the day. We will reconvene here after your next birthday celebration."

"Why?" Chase shouted. "That's months away. There is no reason. We did our jobs. We completed our missions."

"I will return all your assets at that time," Smith said.

"Hell, no!" Nash roared. "I said we shouldn't trust you." He looked around at the group. "Didn't I?"

The guys answered with shrugs and shakes of the head.

"What is the reason?" Beau asked in a calm voice.

"It will make sense in due time."

"Don't start with that crap," Finn called out. "You've been using metaphors and sayings to distract us. Say what you mean, damn it."

"Whoa, look who took up swearing. Does Mommy know?" Nash asked. "If we want someone to cuss him out?" He paused. "Chase, you have the floor."

"Shut up, Nash," Chase growled. "Look, Smith," he said in a calm voice. "You were supposed to return our money when we completed the assignments. Mission accomplished."

"Again, may I reiterate, you will receive your full assets a year from when you gave them to me."

"The transfers didn't happen right away," Beau said. "Our birthday celebration was in March. By the time we received our dossiers and returned them to you, it was April. Some of us didn't get things completed until May."

"You are correct, Mr. Miller. I will see you then."

"Wait!" Kade shouted. "You're not leaving until we're satisfied." He glanced around at the others and said, "I don't know about you guys, but I'm not happy."

The grumblings grew louder until Mr. Smith shouted, "Enough! You young men have learned many things throughout the past weeks. Be grateful for what you have. One thing you did not learn is patience. Patience is a virtue. That is the next lesson. Starting today, you will have access to your accounts, but they remain with me. I am the primary shareholder."

"Smith!" Gabe yelled. "Why do we need another lesson?"

"Is this really happening?" Finn grumbled. "We need more answers."

"We're not in school anymore, Smith," Nash shouted. "We don't need a teacher."

"What the hell is going on? Everyone sit down and let Smith talk," Chase demanded. "Go on, Smith. You were saying?"

The room went silent. Kade held his breath without realizing he was. He let out a loud whoosh of air before he spoke. "I hate to say this, guys. But he did it again. Smith's not here."

"He left?" Nash asked. "Without so much as a goodbye? Typical."

"Let's go out to the man cave," Finn said. "Chase is hoping someone will show up today."

"Not today, Finn," Chase replied. "Tomorrow. I had no idea we'd meet on a Friday."

"Okay, then we'll all wait for this mysterious, special someone to show up tomorrow."

"As long as I'm on a plane by one p.m., I'm in," Kade said. The others agreed they must stay, too.

"Fine," Chase said. "Just don't embarrass me."

CHAPTER NINETEEN

To celebrate their victory, the guys partied late into the night. Smith may still have their money for the time being, but they'd won. Most slept past breakfast the next day, exhausted from the festivities. Kade woke to a phone call from Mia.

"Hi, Mia."

"Hi, how are you?"

"Better now that I hear your voice."

"I won't keep you. I have a favor to ask."

"Ask away." The answer will be yes."

"Can I wait for you at the loft? I want to be there when you come home."

"Sure." Kade rubbed his eyes, trying to wake up.

"How do I get in?"

Kade laughed. "Got a pen? I'll tell you the codes." He rolled from the bed and headed to his bathroom to take a quick shower. Each Society member had their own bedroom and bath at Chase's house, which made things easier when they got together.

Standing in the bathroom, Kade rattled off the codes to get in the building and onto the elevator. Once inside the elevator, Mia needed to punch in another code. "Got it?" he asked.

"Yes, thanks. I'll let you go. What time do you think you'll get home?"

"Late afternoon?" Kade winced, remembering the promise to stick around for Chase's mystery person.

"Okay, I'll see you then."

After Kade had dressed for the day, he headed downstairs to the kitchen. The island held a buffet of food and liquid beverages. "Good morning, Renata." Kade walked to the sink where she stood and kissed her on the cheek. "How do you put up with us?" He winked.

"You are my boys," Renata answered. "I love you all."

The guys trickled in until all six sat at the table in the dinette area next to the kitchen. Chase appeared nervous and hardly ate. When Nash went back for seconds, Kade thought Chase would jump out of his skin.

"Chase," Kade said. "I'm done. If you want to head to the bunker, I'm happy to go with you."

"We'll all be there in a few minutes," Gabe added. "Nash is a fast eater."

Chase nodded at Kade. "If you don't mind?"

"Sure." Kade nudged Nash as he passed by. "Hurry up."

"Hey, I'm trying to eat here." Nash shoved his fork into a pile of scrambled eggs.

Kade smiled and shook his head. He continued out to the patio and followed the path to the bunker. Chase had jogged ahead, unlocking the door for them.

"She must be special," Kade said when he got inside.

"Very." Chase nodded.

The other four Society members arrived as a group. Kade hid a smile, assuming they'd stopped Nash from going back for a third helping. He checked the time, seeing it was almost noon. Chase had scheduled the New York plane to leave at one. He hoped the mysterious guest showed up soon.

Within five minutes, a knock came at the bunker door.

"That must be her," Chase said, hurrying to answer. He'd dressed casually in shorts, t-shirt and sandals, but to Kade, he appeared nervous as hell.

"You came!" Chase said a little too loudly.

"I did." A woman with dark blonde hair looked down at the stone walkway. Chase reached out and pulled her into his arms.

"Oh, baby, I am so sorry I had to leave you. I promise I will answer all your questions if we have to stay up all night."

The woman peered over Chase's shoulder and made eye contact with Kade.

Shocked by who he saw, Kade blinked a few times to make sure. *Grace Edison? Mia's friend?*

"Uh, Chase?" she said.

"Them?" He looked over his shoulder, then whispered in her ear. As they gave each other a passionate kiss for the first time in six weeks, cheers erupted in the room.

Grace leaned back and lifted the front of Chase's hair as if to look for his scar.

"Still there, but the doctor said it should fade in time." Chase placed his arm around her waist and turned her toward the men seated in recliners and on a rounded leather sectional. "Grace? I'd like you to meet my friends, the best guys you'll ever meet. We met in college and have been…"

Someone in the room cleared their throat and Chase shot a look his way as if sending daggers.

"It's nice to meet you all," Grace said, scanning the room to make eye contact with each man.

Chase guided her into the room for introductions. Nash rose from his seat. "Grace, good to see you again."

"I'm not surprised to see you, Nash." Grace smiled.

The couple made the rounds, talking to Finn, Beau, Gabe and finally Kade. "Nice to see you again, too."

"Kade?" Grace touched the area below her neck. Oh, my gosh! Mia's Kade? I can't believe it."

"You two know each other?" Chase asked.

Kade smiled. He thought back to his time at The Pearl when he first met Grace. It had bothered him all weekend. *How did I know that name? Well, I finally got the answer to my question.* "I met Grace in San Francisco last week," he said. "She's friends with my …"

"Girlfriend?" Grace winked.

"Yes." Kade smiled. "My girlfriend."

* * * *

Glad Mia had called him before leaving Charlotte, Kade walked into the loft to find her waiting as promised. A bottle of wine and two glasses sat on the island. Mia was placing a snack on the table as he came toward her.

"Kade, you're back! Thanks for trusting me with your loft code. I wanted to be here when you arrived."

Mia fell into his arms, and Kade grasped her tightly. So many emotions ran through him, he fought to hold them back. He longed to confide in her, let her in on the Society and their business, but they'd pledged secrecy and he had to honor the code.

"So are you a groomsman?" Mia looked up at him with curious eyes.

What? Oh yeah. I lied. "Yes, definitely."

"You didn't tell Nash I knew Vanessa, did you?"

"No, you said you wanted to tell her first."

"Did you plan a couples date?"

"Not yet, but you're in for a surprise. Your friend Grace is Chase's girlfriend."

"What?" Mia wore a look of surprise, then smiled. "It is a small world. *Two* people I know are now with your friends."

"It's a little eerie, isn't it," Kade teased. "It's not like we grew up together or went to the same college. We live in different states. How did we all meet? Wow." He ran his hand over his mouth. "You're right. Small world."

"I was just about to open the bottle of wine," Mia said, guiding Kade to the island.

"I'll do the honors," Kade offered. He pulled the cork from the bottle and poured the liquid into the two glasses. "To us. We are an official couple now."

"I'm excited to be your first girlfriend." Mia fluttered her lashes and laughed. "Oh! I need to make a reservation. I want to take you to this little out of the way place I love. Later. Much later. I want you all to myself for now." She reached for her phone.

Kade watched as she dialed. "Don't they have online reservations?"

"No." Mia shook her head. "They're old school." She held up her pointer finger as the call went through. "Hi, I'd like to make a reservation for seven o'clock tonight. For two. Seven-fifteen? Yes, that's fine. Name? Smith. Mia Smith."

Bells went off in Kade's head. *Smith!* When she hung up, he fought to stay composed and asked, "Do you always give Smith as your last name?"

"It's an old habit. My family has done it forever when they make reservations. It seems Takeda is too hard to spell or something. My dad always uses it."

Her dad? Come to think of it, he avoided me the whole time I was at The Pearl. I never met him. What if he's...

"Kade? Are you okay?"

"Yeah, fine. Can I ask you something?"

"Sure."

"I never met your dad. Did he ask about me? Want to meet me?"

"Let me think." Mia touched her finger to the side of her mouth and looked up at the ceiling. "No, I don't think he ever mentioned you. I wanted him to meet you. Turns out he was very busy that weekend."

Avoiding me. I've got to call Beau. This is the best lead yet. The guy also knows Grace. Does he know Vanessa and the rest of the girls? There's a connection here. Damn, I think I'm on to something. Why did Smith point me in the direction of his daughter? Why me?

"Kade, you're doing it again," Mia touched his arm.

"Sorry."

"We have two and half long hours until we need to leave. I wonder what we should do?" Mia teased him with a coy grin. She rose from her seat and strolled toward his bedroom. When she reached the entryway, she paused and looked over her shoulder as she slipped the spaghetti strap from her sundress off her shoulder. "Oops!"

Heat built inside Kade. If she was trying to distract him, she was doing a good job. All he saw was Mia. She wanted him. Hell, he wanted her more. *What was I thinking about just a minute ago?* He watched her disappear into his bedroom and her sundress came flying out the door. *I have no idea and don't care.*

In five long strides he was at the bedroom door, stopped and leaned against the frame. He loved what he saw. Kade drank in the sight of her. Mia, his Mia, lay on the bed inviting him to join her. *To hell with Smith. To hell with the Society. I am finally happy. I have all I want right here in front of me.*

Kade joined her on his bed and took Mia in his arms, planning to make her his forever.

The End

Preview
The Elusive Mr. Smith – The $ecret
Billionaire $ociety – Book 7
Chapter One

"Everyone! Shut. Up. Now!"

All eyes rested on him. Blurry, blood-shot ones. Half-opened and blinking to stay awake eyes. One pair, not surprisingly, clear and awake.

If they say I'm their leader then I need to do something about this mess. Chase cleared his throat. "We are here to celebrate our thirty-first birthdays, not throw accusations at each other."

After his statement, chaos ensued again with major finger pointing.

"Look!" Chase held up his hands. "I am trying not to swear here. I promised Grace I'd work on my "f" bombs and everything in between. But, damn, guys, what's happened to us? This is the first time all of us have been together in more than a year. Fourteen months since we found Mr. Smith. Because he still owns our holdings, we agreed to celebrate in May so we could discuss his change in plans. Arguing won't get us anywhere."

"We're not arguing, buddy. We *are* discussing." Nash winked. Out of all the Society members, Nash had the most laid-back attitude and found humor in most everything until their mission. He still had his jokester side but had grown more serious. Chase thought it was a good thing since Nash planned to marry his longtime girlfriend in July.

"Let's discuss." Chase turned to Beau, the level-headed, cyber security master and all-round good guy. "Beau, a plan?"

Beau pointed to himself. "You want me to make a plan?"

"I believe I just said that." Chase smiled, trying to send a telepathic message to the man. He needed help.

"Okay, give me a minute to think on it," Beau said, bringing his hand to his chin. "Last night we agreed to put all questions pertaining to Mr. Smith aside until this morning. Instead of discussing things in a sane manner, it's turned into a free for all. My suggestion?" He raised his brows. "We take turns speaking our piece."

"Or forever hold it," Nash chimed in.

Beau ignored him and continued. "Chase, you go first. I'll take notes."

"Not fair," Nash shouted. "Let's draw straws or something. Rock, paper, scissors, anyone?"

"Nash." Beau stared at his best friend. "We'll all get our turn. Sit down, be quiet and listen."

When they first met, Nash called Beau 'stuffed shirt' and Beau named him 'muscles'. They swore they'd get new roommates winter semester and pledged to tolerate each other until then. It had happened slowly and before they knew it, they realized they were yin and yang, the last two pieces to the puzzle, peanut butter and jelly and became inseparable.

"Beau, did anyone ever tell you, you're no fun?" Nash slumped back in his chair.

"Yes, you. Many times." Beau chuckled. "After Chase speaks, we'll decide who goes next. Coffee anyone?"

Chase smiled. *Leave it to Beau to make everyone change direction by offering them coffee.* Most got up from their seats and wandered over to the long table which held food and drink. Chase had a breakfast buffet brought in to feed the guys. Easy to do since they were close to many hotels and restaurants.

They usually held their birthday celebrations in exotic locations or on a yacht off a Caribbean island. This time they'd chosen closer to home, or Chase's house, where they could still go to the beach and golf. Chase had rented an oceanfront property with eight bedrooms and six baths in Hilton Head, South Carolina. It came with its own pool, jacuzzi, tiki bar and private beach. They made good use of them last night, yet it didn't seem the same. Aware it wasn't the usual birthday blowout, Chase hoped it still gave the feeling of a celebration.

Chase took a breath and waited for the guys to return from the buffet. The last one straggled in and found a seat. He paced in front of them, sprawled in various positions on the sunroom's furniture, resting plates on their stomachs or laps.

"I want to start from the beginning," Chase said. "Let's walk through this together, one step at a time." He drew in a breath, tapped his fingertips together as he let it out. "Last March we met in Hawaii for our thirtieth birthday celebration like we've done since we graduated from Harvard. The Secret Billionaire Society swore to help each other until we made our money and beyond. We achieved the goal. We became billionaires, each one of us. You all have made The Forbes top 100 list, and some have become one of the top ten billionaires in the country." He glanced at Beau, whose dream was to become one of the top ten U.S. black billionaires. This was the third year he made the list. He nodded at him in acknowledgment.

"We got pretty drunk that night." Chase smiled. "Someone had gotten melancholy and asked if this was all there was to life—partying, drinking and making money. Nash stood, beer in hand, and gave quite the speech about the qualities of those three things. As I recall, a giant wrestling match took place to shut him up."

"I believe it was you who asked the question, Chase," Finn announced. "Is that all there is?" he sang the words as he gazed at the ceiling.

"Very funny. I could have." Chase looked at his best friend and his college roommate. Tan and fit, blonde hair and blue eyes, he was the perfect-looking California boy. They couldn't be more opposite. Chase from meager beginnings in life and Finn from a wealthy real estate family. Yet, if not for Finn's connections, none of them would have made their money so quickly. It could have taken decades. The guys gave credit to Chase's investing skills, but he needed their money first. None of them came from wealth except Finn. Finn had contacts and people to go to for advice. It became their springboard, a jumping off place to start their careers.

"Once we decided we wanted to do something for the greater good, we," Chase said, waving his hand around in the air. "Fell down this rabbit hole we called Mission Impossible. We wanted someone to give us our assignments, a person we'd never see. Like in the show."

"The man behind the mirror," Finn called to him.

"Yes, Smith became the man behind the mirror." Chase nodded. "He instructed us to build a place, a two-room soundproof dwelling. I volunteered my property where there was enough space for the bunker and special driveway. Mr. Smith could slip into an entrance directly connected to the darkened side of the one-way mirror room without being seen, and we'd sit on the other."

"The mancave is the still best part of the bunker." Nash shrugged. "Just saying."

"We can't be serious all the time, can we? I felt we needed it." Chase lifted a corner of his mouth. "Okay, back to our timeline. We sent our dossiers to Smith and built the bunker. Those things took over two months. Our first meeting with Smith was in June."

"Where he chose you to go first, bro," Finn said. "And we're glad he did."

"And we know how that ended,' Chase answered.

"Grace!" The other five shouted.

"Yes, I met Grace, but I also saved her father's airline. That was the idea, wasn't it? Help someone in need."

"You could have died helping them, Chase," Gabe said in a serious tone. His eyes appeared clear and bright when he connected with Chase's. "Someone tampered with your brakes and you ended up in the hospital. If we ever meet Smith, I'll happily remind him that he almost killed you."

"I'm fine." Chase spread out his arms. "See? No harm done."

"You're too forgiving," Gabe replied. "Look at Nash. Smith almost got Vanessa killed during his mission."

Chase paused to think. Gabe was dwelling on the negatives and had seemed anxious since his arrival to Hilton Head. He wondered what was going on with his friend. *Work? Not Lily. Gabe's never been happier since he and his longtime friend became a couple.*

Founder of Nicholworks, a creative tech company, Gabe resided in Boulder, Colorado. He and Kade were the only two of the Society who knew each other before Harvard. They'd been the last two to join The Secret Billionaire Society, which Chase and Finn had started as a joke in college.

Gabe had questioned Mission Impossible from the start, and it might be the reason he'd kept track of the bad things that happened during their assignments. But Chase had to give it to him. Gabe was right. Smith put some people in danger. He hadn't planned it, but things went sideways.

"You're right, Gabe," Chase said. "We need to acknowledge the bad with the good. Nash's assignment turned darker than we thought. I'm sure Smith didn't see it coming either. No one expected those bastards to kidnap Vanessa." He waited for Gabe to respond. When he didn't, he continued. "Now that our missions are over, we have more questions than answers. That's why we're here. To figure it out. During our assignments, some of us got clues to Smith's identity. Others learned more after they completed their missions. I discovered Grace and Mia knew each other after Kade finished his mission. Is there a connection? Or is it coincidence?" He looked at Kade.

"I can't say." Kade lifted his shoulders. "Mia knows Vanessa, too. She met Van her freshman year at Florida State. They roomed together."

"Since we're talking about my girl, I'd like to say something," Nash said then looked at Chase. "If you're done."

"For now, yes." Chase turned to Beau. "It's up to you."

"Nash can go next," Beau stated with a nod.

* * * *

"Thanks, bro." Nash stood in front of the group. All eyes were on him. "You guys think I work out all day and do nothing else. Not true. Yeah, I own some awesome gyms and dedicate lots of time to them, but I've thought about this Smith thing, too. I agree with our final conclusion. This was personal to him. Our assignments weren't random acts of kindness that some guy pulled out of a hat. Smith had a plan *way* before he met us. We came along at the right time. He used us to further his agenda. I believe Mia, Van and/or Grace know this person. I'm also adding Tess to the equation, Beau. You mentioned her grandmother had a connection to the man."

Nash shrugged. "That's all I got on Smith, but I have more to say." He took a breath and slowly let it out. "Van and I have been together for years. You knuckleheads are now in relationships. Good ones. Ones I hope last. But did I ever let mine get in the way of friendship? I came to every party, every business meeting and every celebration we had. This is the first time all of us have been in the same room since our final Smith meeting last July. Something's got to give. We're *the* Six. The Secret Billionaire Society. I'm not giving up that easily."

"No one is giving up, Nash," Beau said. "True, our lives have changed since last summer. We've been caught up in the moment, but no one feels any different about the Society. We still see each other."

"We get together," Nash acknowledged. "But as couples. Van and I went out with Kade and Mia. You and Tess have flown down to see us in Florida. New Year's everyone went to Boulder to stay with Gabe and Lily except Chase and me."

"I invited you. You couldn't get away for the entire week and chose not to come," Gabe replied. "You, too, Chase."

"Okay, I'll give you that." Nash rubbed the stubble on his chin. "Chase and Grace flew down to Miami Beach for a quick celebration with us. But we've never done that before. We're either all together or stay in our home states." Nash shook his head. "Hell, the girls are making more of an effort than us. They text, call and get together on their own."

"I, for one, am glad they are friends," Kade said. "They were very understanding about our birthday celebration."

"Because they're flying to San Francisco for a girls' weekend and the memorial for Sean O'Donnell." Nash widened his eyes and lifted his hands in the air. "We picked this weekend because it suddenly opened up and became convenient."

Mia Takeda and Grace Edison had become friends through their connection to Mia's cousin, Sean. Grace met him at college, they became a couple and he'd bring her home on holidays. Mia and Grace bonded immediately and knew they'd be friends for life. Tragically struck by a car the night he proposed to Grace, Sean died instantly. The family had a memorial for him every year to commemorate his spirit.

"The women are on one of Chase's private jets flying to San Francisco for the memorial as we speak," Nash continued. "All of us expect a text within the next few hours to say they safely landed. Which is great. We love them. I think we need to make more of an effort to get together like they do. That's all. I've said my piece. I'll sit down and shut up." Nash started for his chair.

"No, wait." Finn held up his hand. "You're right, Nash. We haven't been totally present. We've only thought of ourselves and our new relationships. Guys," he said, glancing around the room. "Don't you agree?'

Four heads nodded. "You make sense, Nash," Beau said. "I'm sorry."

"Eh, you don't need to apologize," Nash responded.

"I think we do. You made your point, Nash," Kade said.

"What about your wedding?" Finn asked. "Are you still getting married in July? We need to discuss details."

So they do care. Nash smiled. "Thanks for asking, Finn. Van would beat my ass if she knew I never brought it up. In fact, she plans to ask the girls to be part of the wedding party this weekend. She has too many cousins and doesn't want to hurt any feelings. Van asked her sister, Rosa, to be her matron of honor and I've asked Beau to be my best man. Rosa's husband will round out the guys' side. Only Beau and he will switch partners. They rest of you dorks will partner with your significant other."

"Mia's been acting very strange for a few weeks. I think she knew," Kade said. "Van asked her to design her wedding gown, but she's been sketching all hours of the day and night. Now it makes sense. She's doing all the dresses. I'm proud of her. We're spinning her off into her own wedding brand called *Simply Mia.*"

"How does Jor*dan* like that?" Nash asked with a chuckle.

"He's fine, especially since they called their brand Jor*dan* and Mia. With a capital D." Kade winked. "Congrats, bro. Speaking for the rest of the guys." He glanced around the group. "We're honored to be in your wedding. And…" He paused, looking around the room and gave a nod. "It's about damn time you married Vanessa."

The guys leaped from their seats and pounced on Nash. Knuckles rubbed his scalp. Someone kissed him on the cheek. Arms wrapped around his waist to lift him in the air. Voices shouted congratulations and outlandish, crude words he wouldn't want his parents to hear. "Enough," Nash shouted, laughing so hard his sides hurt.

Once everyone stepped away, Nash let out a long breath. "I love you, guys. You're the best." He paused then yelled, "Six!"

"From the bottom to the top!" they shouted their motto and came together to join hands in a pyramid, their secret symbol.

"And now, back to our previously scheduled show." Nash swept his hand across his waist and bowed. "I give the floor to…" He studied each face and came to rest on the one he wanted to feel included. The guy who acted like he didn't belong, when he deserved to be in the group maybe more than the others. Quiet, yet thoughtful. Tough in a fight. "Gabe!" he exclaimed.

* * * *

Really? My turn already? I didn't expect it to go like this. I thought I'd be last. I always am. Gabe looked at Beau to seek permission.

"You have the floor, my man." Beau lifted a brow. "You okay?"

"Yeah, I'm fine." Gabe waited until the guys took their seats. "You may or may not know that Beau, Kade and I have kept a list on Smith clues. If not, I'm telling you now. There's a list and you're welcomed to add to it. I believe Smith has had me on his radar for a while because of Blair. In case you forgot, she's my ex from high school. You know the story. She came to town, tried to con me into thinking her son was mine for money. Which wasn't true. River wasn't my son."

"Of course not. Blair's always been good at lying," Kade said in a show of solidarity. The two went way back, friends since they were ten years old.

"Smith must have some kind of agency watching people like Blair and her dad," Gabe continued. "Dave Winters was a con artist in his younger days and after his divorce from Blair's mom, he went back to his old ways. Except this time, he pulled Blair into his schemes and used her as bait. I think Smith was watching them for a long time. He must have built a file on them and I'm positive my name's in there."

"Wait a minute." Finn raised his hand. "You think Smith knew who we were, or at least you, before we contacted him?"

"Yes." Gabe nodded. "Somehow he knew Blair would come for me."

"This is creepy. Like Big Brother is watching," Nash said with a fake shiver. "When we find this guy, he's got a lot of explaining to do."

"Now that I've told my story, I have an announcement." Gabe closed his eyes and pulled together all the strength he could manage. "I quit. I quit The Secret Billionaire Society. I'm out."

What happens next? Find out in Book 7
The Elusive Mr. Smith: The Secret Billionaire Society
Always free on Kindle Unlimited

The $ecret Billionaire $ociety
(Contemporary Romantic Suspense)

Chase (Book 1)

Nash (Book 2)

Finn (Book 3)

Beau (Book 4)

Gabe (Book 5)

Kade (Book 6)

The Elusive Mr. Smith (Book 7)

Smith's Revenge (Book 8)

BEFORE YOU GO

THANK YOU FOR READING

Did you enjoy this book?
I invite you to leave a review at your favorite book site, such as
Goodreads, BookBub and Amazon.

DID YOU KNOW THAT LEAVING A REVIEW...

Helps other readers find books they may enjoy.
Gives you a chance to let your voice be heard.
Gives authors recognition for their hard work.

Doesn't have to be long. A sentence or two about why you liked the book will do.

OTHER BOOKS BY NANCY PENNICK

Waiting for Dusk Series (Young Adult)

Waiting for Dusk (Book 1)

Call of The Canyon (Book 2)

Stealing Time (Book 3)

Taking Chances (Short Story)

Broken Dreams (Prequel)

Twenty Nine Series (Young Adult)

29

29 Squared

29 Degrees

29 Forever

The Clan MacLaren Series
(Historical Romance)

My Highlander Husband (Book 1)

Donnach's Daughter (Book 2)

The Heart of the Emerald (Book 3)

Now and Forever (Book 4)

MacLaren Strong (Book 5)

Homecoming (Book 6)

ABOUT THE AUTHOR

Nancy Pennick, author of young adult and romance books, has been writing nonstop since retiring from teaching. Starting off as a young adult author, she has enjoyed diving into other genres. In other words, she likes to write whatever comes to mind! Born and raised in Northeast Ohio, she resides in Mentor, OH. Nancy is married and has one son.